YA Spinne
Spinner, Stephanie
Quiver /

34028081804420
CC $5.99   ocm59005835
             09/12/13

HARRIS COUNTY PUBLIC LIBRARY

W9-BEC-899

for Stephanie Spinner's *Quiver*

"In an elegant trajectory, *Quiver* links the mythic past with modern young readers in this sensuous story of the alluring, timeless Atalanta."

—Richard Peck, Newbery Medalist for *A Year Down Yonder*

"Spinner gives this Greek myth a fresh face . . . a fine introduction to the Greek tales."   —*School Library Journal*

"Stephanie Spinner evokes ancient Greece with such a sure hand that she might have been there herself. *Quiver* is a subtle, seamless work about a time full of soul and mystery."

—Steven Pressfield, author of *Last of the Amazons*

"*Quiver* has it all: spiteful gods, revenge, humor, romance, suspense, and a startling ending. Stephanie Spinner's brilliant retelling of the legend of Atalanta reminds you why the Greek myths are still the best stories in the world."

—Gloria Whelan, winner of the National Book Award for *Homeless Bird*

"Beautifully rendered."   —*The San Jose Mercury News*

ALSO AVAILABLE FROM DELL LAUREL-LEAF BOOKS

GODDESS OF YESTERDAY, Caroline B. Cooney

THE GREAT GOD PAN, Donna Jo Napoli

THE LEGEND OF LADY ILENA, Patricia Malone

BEOWULF: A NEW TELLING, Robert Nye

THE DARK HORSE, Marcus Sedgwick

THE HEALER'S KEEP, Victoria Hanley

HEROES, GODS AND MONSTERS OF
THE GREEK MYTHS, Bernard Evslin

GREEK GODS AND HEROES, Robert Graves

QUIVER

STEPHANIE SPINNER

Published by
Dell Laurel-Leaf
an imprint of
Random House Children's Books
a division of Random House, Inc.
New York

If you purchased this book without a cover you should be aware that
this book is stolen property. It was reported as "unsold and destroyed"
to the publisher and neither the author nor the publisher has received
any payment for this "stripped book."

Text copyright © 2002 by Stephanie Spinner
Cover design copyright © 2002 by Alfred A. Knopf
Map illustration copyright © 2002 by Tony Morse

All rights reserved. No part of this book may be reproduced or
transmitted in any form or by any means, electronic or mechanical,
including photocopying, recording, or by any information storage and
retrieval system, without the written permission of the publisher, except
where permitted by law. For information address Alfred A. Knopf.

Dell and Laurel are registered trademarks of Random House, Inc.

Visit us on the Web! www.randomhouse.com/teens

Educators and librarians, for a variety of teaching tools, visit us at
www.randomhouse.com/teachers

ISBN: 0-440-23819-6

RL: 5.8

Reprinted by arrangement with Alfred A. Knopf

Printed in the United States of America

First Dell Laurel-Leaf Edition April 2005

10 9 8 7 6 5

OPM

For Megan Parry Brill

CONTENTS

When I was an infant, abandoned in the forest, Artemis the Huntress sent a she-bear to nurse me. Soon after, a band of hunters found me—naked, kicking, and slick with bear grease. Knowing that only Artemis would save an infant girl in the wild and eager to win the goddess's favor, the hunters took me in.

As soon as I could walk, they taught me to hold a bow. On the day of my first kill, they told me how the stern, beautiful goddess had saved my life and showed me how to offer to her. I did this solemnly, for I had long imagined her as my mother— distant, yes, but strong and radiant as the moon. I knew her love was bound to shine on me again, if only I were content to wait.

So I did.

PART ONE

The Hunt

The caw of a crow warned me first. Then it was their smell—so rank it made my eyes water.

I had never been so close to centaurs before, though of course I had seen them. There were many in my native Arcadia—wild, filthy creatures, notorious for their lack of restraint, and far more dangerous than satyrs. When they drank—as they often did, to excess—they would rape and beat whatever women they could find, which was why women never ventured into the forests alone.

I am not alone, I reminded myself, I am with the Hunt, in Calydon.

Yet the centaurs were at hand, and the other hunters were too far off to be of help, should I cry out.

I would not; I would rather die.

They came at a gallop, legs churning, chests heaving.

I could run as swiftly as they. Indeed, I could outrun most creatures, human or otherwise. But there were two of them, and they were lust-maddened.

I drew my bow.

On they came, one with a torn ear, the other with a bulbous, red-veined nose. They were large and coarse and frightening, with none of the capering insolence that made their goat brothers almost endearing. Both had rough piebald coats, long, matted tails, and hooves as big as mallets.

Their stink was fearsome.

I shot the one with the red nose first. He reared. I hit him again, and he fell, snorting blood. I loosed two arrows, then three, at the other. He was so close when he toppled that I could feel his heat. He cursed me, groaning and choking. I backed away. They were huge creatures, and their great hooves kicked out as they died.

"Safe crossing," I whispered.

Then I heard a soft whistle that rose and fell like a question—Meleager, looking for me.

I signaled back and he emerged through the trees. As I moved toward him, I saw the concern in his dark eyes fade, and he smiled broadly.

He is relieved, I thought, knowing it was more than relief that lit up his face. We had met only days before, when the Hunt assembled at his father's palace, and since then Meleager had paid me many small courtesies—inquiring after my comfort whenever we chanced to meet, asking my opinion of his weaponry, introducing me to his beloved hounds. I required no more than any of the men, yet he sought me out time after time.

I was flattered by his interest, for I liked him. He was straightforward and guileless, a man who preferred his hounds to his father's courtiers. He was a decent hunter, too—very good with the javelin, and passable with a bow. The dark stories about his fate—some said he carried a birth curse—made me feel a kind of kinship with him.

Nevertheless, I had no desire for romantic entanglements. Like the men, I was here for glory. Moreover, I had taken a vow of chastity in honor of Artemis, and I intended to keep it. Seeing the yearning in Meleager's eyes, I resolved to tell him of my vow as soon as I could.

I raised a finger in warning. I had lost the boar's scent, but he was cunning, and might be nearby. The sight of the slain centaurs stopped Meleager, but when he looked at me inquiringly I shook my head; explanations would have to come later. I started back up the hillside and he followed.

Before long we could hear the others thrashing through the trees. Then all twenty-seven members of the Calydonian Boar Hunt came marching downhill in crescent formation, armed to the eyebrows. No living thing in the forest could miss hearing them, or seeing them, either. They moved without stealth, as if they were storming the walls of some hapless enemy city.

I was certain that the boar would attack soon, and now, as the great hunt party advanced, I knew I had missed the chance to flush him out myself. I might have done it, I thought, if not for those stinking centaurs. They had likely cost me the head and pelt, and now the prizes of the hunt would go to one of the men. More than half of them were Argonauts—the intrepid, battle-scarred band who had sailed with Jason in search of the Golden Fleece. The adventure had made them heroes, and in the manner of heroes, each one of them considered victory his due.

"Why did you leave?" whispered Meleager.

"I smelled him—" Then it came again, a heavy mix of smoke and fat and marshland mud, and with it, tremors like those that shake the earth before it rips apart. He was very near.

The hounds bayed. Then one of them screamed—a death cry. Meleager froze. His Laconian hounds were very dear to him.

"There!" I pointed to a place fifty paces off.

He was bigger than a bull, with bristles like skewers and filthy tusks as long as javelins. Steam came off his body like the foul nimbus of some underworld being; even in morning light, he seemed to stand in gloom. The hound on his tusk was dead, and he rid himself of it impatiently, tossing his massive head and stamping so that the ground shook. Then he wheeled—swiftly for all his bulk—to regard us with eyes as small and red as pomegranate seeds. It was the look of a beast without predators, who had never felt fear.

My arrow was nocked, but Echion ran at the boar shouting, and when he flung his spear, I hesitated. Even as the spear fell short, the boar charged. Echion's twin, Erytus, along with Jason, Eupalamus, and Iphicles, scrambled away as the creature hurtled at them like a rock from a catapult, crushing everything in its path. It trampled hounds, flattened trees, and flung Eupalamus and Iphicles aside as if they were made of straw.

Then Jason threw, but his spear went wide. He flattened himself on the ground, drawing his great shield over him as if he were a giant tortoise. Erytus was nimble also, using his long spear to vault out of the beast's way, and landing in a tree. Young Hippasus lacked the experience—and the luck—of his comrades; the boar veered suddenly and gored him before he could escape. He fell and lay still, arms and legs askew.

Undaunted, Mopsus rushed forward. It was said he was gifted with the Sight, and could understand the language of the birds. Now he cried out to Apollo, Lord of the Silver Bow.

"If I have been your faithful worshiper, great Apollo," he cried, "grant me good aim!" He must have been heard; his spear flew straight and true.

Indeed, it should have killed the boar. Yet its jagged iron head came off in flight, and when its wooden shaft hit the boar's neck, it bounced to the ground as harmlessly as a broom handle.

Meleager hissed in amazement.

The boar grunted, flicking its tail.

An all-consuming lightness, like heatless fever, came over me. My skin prickled as if a storm were coming, and my hearing grew so acute that I imagined I could hear the slow lap and surge of blood under my skin. I knew the signs; I had known them since girlhood.

The goddess, I thought. She is here.

Apollo had heard Mopsus. But Artemis, who had sent the boar to plague King Oeneus for failing to sacrifice to her, even now intervened.

Goddess, I am yours, I murmured. If it pleases you, guide my hand.

The boar lowered its head to charge at Mopsus, and at that instant my shot came clear. Flying as if Artemis herself had loosed it, my arrow struck the boar's neck and pierced its bristled hide. Blood spurted where it hit. Whispering my thanks, I flushed with pleasure; there was honor in drawing first blood.

The beast shook its massive head, but the arrow stuck. Mopsus fled as the boar danced in fury, squealing.

"Do you see?" cried Meleager. His voice thrilled with

such emotion that the shot might have been his. "Atalanta has hit the boar!"

Apollo: You might have let Mopsus take that shot, you know. He did invoke me.

Artemis: Yes, but she's been praying to me for weeks. I had to give it to her.

Apollo: Are you going to help her kill it, too? That would certainly cause an uproar.

Artemis: It would. But there are other, even more interesting possibilities. And the hunt is far from over.

Apollo: You frighten me sometimes.

Artemis: I'm your older sister. I probably should.

TWO

Some on the Hunt objected to my presence, whispering that it would bring misfortune. Others simply stared at me as if I were a white crow, or a three-legged heifer.

For all its prowess, it was a rude bunch.

But I was used to such behavior, and to biding my time until a moment like this, when my shot hit home. It gave me joy to see the beast retreat, smashing into a thicket with my arrow piercing its neck, but I did not show it. Instead, I kept my face blank—a skill honed by years of practice— and sent another prayer of thanks to the goddess.

"Well done!" cried Meleager. Jason raised his eyebrows at me, smiling his wry smile. He always enjoyed the surprise of others when they first witnessed my skill with a bow, though few reacted with as much pleasure as Meleager. The usual response was a mixture of disbelief and indignation, which Jason found comical. I forgave him because he was a brotherly friend of long standing, and because he truly respected my shooting. He had once said that I could win against anyone, even the greatest archers in Hellas, if such a contest were ever held. I treasured the remark.

Ancaeus scowled and muttered something to Cepheus. The two were Arcadian, as I was, yet I felt no bond with them. Cepheus was a bully, a big man who walked with his jaw jutting out, as if challenging the world to disagree with him. Ancaeus was a braggart, even bigger and louder than Cepheus. Worse, he went about in a bearskin. A bear had saved my life, so I disliked Ancaeus as much for his cloak as for his bad character.

They had no affection for me, either. In their view, women were creatures of servitude, best kept hobbled. I had outrun and outshot them both, and this lack of deference they found impossible to forgive. They would not so much as acknowledge me on the tiny raft that took us from

Achaea to Aetolia, and when the Hunt assembled before King Oeneus the following day, they threatened to leave if I did not. A woman had no place on the expedition, Ancaeus had growled, looking around the hall for assent. There were a few barely perceptible nods, but no man there was stupid enough to voice his agreement. To do so would surely anger Meleager, to judge by his frown, and possibly the king.

Oeneus had replied dourly that they could stay or go as they wished, it did not matter to him. So they had stayed, losing face, and disliking me even more.

Now Ancaeus brandished his big two-edged ax. "Here is a man's weapon," he shouted, "not some girl's puny arrow! No goddess can protect the boar from this!"

I was aghast. Ancaeus could say what he liked about me, but insulting the goddess was reckless beyond measure. She was quick to take offense, and even quicker to take revenge. I thought of Actaeon, a young hunter who had glimpsed Artemis bathing with her nymphs. He had not meant to see her naked; yet she was the last thing he saw as a man. Enraged that her modesty had been compromised, she changed him into a stag. His own hounds brought him down and mauled him to death. Then, howling inconsolably at what they had done, they died of grief.

"Ancaeus—" I began fearfully.

He glared in my direction, then bellowed, "Make way for me!"

The boar burst from the thicket, hitting Ancaeus in the groin with such force that he rose up, arms outstretched, as if offering to the gods. Thrust aloft, rocked this way and that on the beast's long, bloody tusks, he went to his death wide-eyed, without uttering another word.

I shuddered.

When Ancaeus fell, Meleager's two uncles hurried forward, pointing their spears at the boar. But Plexippus tripped on a root, waylaying Toxeus, and the two men went down, clearing a path for their nephew. He placed his javelin precisely—almost thoughtfully—in the very center of the boar's right side, and it sank in up to the wings. Excellent shot, I thought. The boar shrieked, whirling, and Meleager struck again, this time driving a long spear deep into its breast.

Plexippus and Toxeus scrambled to their feet. Jason approached, spear upraised. But there was no need for another blow; the boar was weaving now, spewing foam flecked with blood. At last it toppled, making a sound like a harsh sob.

At this, many drew near, though slowly. Mopsus knelt at the boar's head, awestruck. Cepheus spat, then turned away with a curse. Lynceus, Iphicles, Echion, and Erytus, all Argonauts, stood together over it, murmuring that it was even uglier than the serpent that had guarded the Fleece. None of them would touch the boar, though Jason dipped his spear in its brown, viscous blood.

One by one, the rest followed suit. I stayed back. I alone had used a bow.

"Someone should take Ancaeus' ax to its head," said Jason, looking around.

16

"I will," said Cepheus grimly. He severed the head with half a dozen ferocious blows of his friend's weapon. Then he laid the ax on the ground, drew out his dagger, and set to flaying the body. It was slow work, but he shook his head at offers of help.

As we stood watching, Jason said to Meleager, "Your father will be doubly pleased."

"Doubly?" said Meleager absently. He was intent on Cepheus' progress.

"That it is dead," said Jason, "and that you killed it. His face will be something to see when you present him with the head and pelt. Who knows? Perhaps he will even smile."

King Oeneus had always been a man of few words. He had grown even gloomier since the autumn, when his over-sight—he had forgotten to sacrifice to Artemis after the harvest—was followed by the appearance of the boar in his kingdom. It caused such havoc that many believed the goddess had sent it to Calydon.

17

Rather than admitting his mistake and offering to her generously, Oeneus had called the hunt. Now the mangled fruits of it lay at our feet.

"That honor will go to Atalanta," said Meleager, looking at me with such ardor that my stomach dropped.

"What!" Jason's exclamation came with a snort of disbelief.

"She was the first to draw blood," said Meleager.

"But you killed it. Everyone saw." Jason spoke slowly, as if to a child.

"No matter," said Meleager, his dark eyes on me. "I want her to have the spoils. And it is my right to give them," he added, lest Jason forget that Meleager was both the host and the king's son.

"Oh . . . no," I stammered, "I cannot accept them." Dismay made my voice shrill, and louder than it should have been. Now Toxeus and Plexippus were listening. Cepheus, whose blood-bespattered face had remained expressionless until this moment, put down his dagger. His mouth hung open in an astonished sneer. I dreaded what he would say.

"Keep them, Meleager," said Jason quietly. "It will only cause bad feeling if you do not."

The prince said nothing. He had a streak of his father's stubbornness. Jason looked at me pointedly, prompting me to speak.

"Yes, keep them," I said, "please, Meleager. They are of no use to me." I spoke as if the words came easily, but they did not. No woman had ever taken such a prize before— won in the company of heroes, awarded by a king—and I truly yearned for it. But Jason was right. The others would take offense if Meleager had his way.

The prince refused to heed us. "You shall have them," he insisted. Jason sighed in exasperation.

After a sudden, heavy silence, Cepheus jumped to his feet, gripping Ancaeus' ax. "You insult us if you do this," he snarled at Meleager. "The dead most of all!"

Meleager's hand went to his scabbard. "And you forget yourself, Cepheus," he replied.

"No, nephew," said Toxeus, stepping in front of Cepheus. "It is you who forget yourself. You are the son of a king, yet this woman"—he pointed his chin at me—"has you playing the dunce."

"Uncle—" Meleager began warningly.

"A slut with dirt between her toes?" added Plexippus. He was the coarser of the queen's two brothers and had been eyeing me since my arrival. "Surely her favors can't be worth the trophies."

Meleager's dagger was in his hand. He looked at his uncles with loathing. "Do not say another word," he warned. "Or I will forget that you are my kin."

"Meleager, please," I said, just as Jason took hold of Meleager's arm. Perhaps it was Cepheus, lurching forward with the ax upraised, or Toxeus, reaching out in a clumsy attempt to snatch Meleager's dagger, or even Jason, shifting like a wrestler, to block him. Yet something ignited Meleager's smoldering rage, and like a torch roaring into flame, or the sweep of fire through dry grass, it consumed them all with terrible swiftness.

I saw a tangle of bodies grappling and falling and coming apart, as one man struck another, and was struck in turn. Jason shouted and broke away with a gash across his arm. Toxeus sank to his knees clutching his chest, blood striping his hands. Then Plexippus pitched forward onto his brother; Meleager's dagger had found him, too.

When it was over, Meleager had wounded a friend and killed two kinsmen. The sun beat down on us with sudden white heat. Meleager turned to me almost blindly.

Mouth dry, I backed away from him.

"Take the trophies," he said.

Apollo: Enough bloodshed!
Artemis: Do you think so?

Apollo: I wish you were more moderate, sister.

Artemis: That's your specialty, not mine. Besides, Oeneus hasn't learned his lesson. What a balky old man he is!

Apollo: Haven't you punished him enough?

Artemis: Others will help me now.

Apollo: What do you mean by that?

Artemis: Wait and see.

THREE

Cepheus bolted, shouting curses. I bound up Jason's torn arm. Then we set off for the palace, with Toxeus' and Plexippus' bodies tied to one shield and the boar's head and hide lashed to another.

It was a searing morning. The air pulsed with heat that grew more intense as we came down from the hills. No wind stirred, and the sun blazed at us in white-hot rebuke. Meleager had gone ahead, leaving me at the rear, and I took some comfort in this. His sudden, brutal rage had shocked me so that I could scarcely meet his eyes.

I walked with Mopsus and Iphicles, who pulled the shields, trailed by a chorus of flies as persistent as the Furies. In the oppressively still air, my head ached and I itched with sweat, which trickled down my face and neck and into my wrist guard. My bow, normally so wieldy, was now burdensome, and my quiver strap chafed. I began to pray for a breeze.

When the long line of huntsmen stopped briefly and I saw Meleager sending two men ahead, I was stupidly pleased. Good! I thought. Now Oeneus will know we are coming.

Forgetting for a moment the cruel events of the morning, I thought only of being welcomed back to the palace with food and drink and clean robes. I imagined the shadowy coolness of the women's bath, with its rush mats and lavender-scented pool, and resolved to offer to the goddess after I had cleansed myself. As for the dull, metallic ache at the back of my throat, I put it down to thirst, for I had not yet learned to recognize the taste of disaster.

Then it happened, in a grove of pines near the palace road. Because I was at the rear I did not see Meleager stop, or begin to hop from foot to foot, as if the pine needles were hot coals. Nor did I see the way he twisted and whirled in a kind of jerky, lunatic dance as the pain intensified.

At first I heard a few voices raised in confusion, and then shouts; I thought one was Meleager's. Mopsus gasped loudly, his face contorting, and the line of men broke apart and ran downhill toward the trees.

"What?" I cried, but the Sight had shown Mopsus something so terrible that he could not speak. Seeing his face twisted with woe, I was seized by panic and ran.

I was the first to reach the grove.

I found Meleager writhing on the ground, covered in pine needles. His hounds crouched nearby, ears flared, whimpering. Jason was backing away from the prince with a look of disbelieving horror on his face.

"No!" groaned Meleager as I ran to him with my arms outstretched. "Do not touch me!"

By then I could feel the heat, waves of it, and see the blisters bubbling up on him as if he were aboil from within.

The sweat on his face steamed; patches of his skin had started to blacken. I wanted to recoil from the stench; instead, I forced myself to draw closer so I could hear what he was trying to say. Eyes rolling, he gasped that it was his mother, the queen, that she had set him afire.

I screamed in vain for water.

He died telling me he loved me.

Apollo: Are you quite finished?

Artemis: Not quite. Nearly.

Jason went into the palace; I could not bear to. Later he told me that when the bodies of her son, Meleager, and her brothers, Plexippus and Toxeus, were borne inside, Queen Althea killed herself with a dagger. Then King Oeneus fell, clutching his heart.

As the king lay on his bed wheezing, a trio of fat, speckled birds waddled into his chamber. They surrounded him, gabbling and pecking at his hands until he died. It was said that this, too, was Artemis' doing, that in a final, vengeful flourish, she had changed the king's three daughters—his last remaining children—into guinea hens.

So ended Oeneus' royal line.

FOUR

I have known Jason since I was a gangly twelve-year-old, from a time before his exploits, his marriage, and his fame. He appeared in our settlement one day wearing a leather tunic, a leopard skin, and one sandal. His fair hair hung loose to his shoulders, and there were strange markings on his forearms, dark blue crosses and snakes. I had never seen such a man, and could hardly keep my eyes on my gluepot. Back then I helped Castor with the simpler tasks of bowyering, like scraping sinew and mixing glue.

Jason greeted Castor by saying that he had come all the way from Iolcus.

"Iolcus? In Thessaly?" replied Castor mildly. Thessaly was many days' journey from Arcadia. None of us had ever been there. To me it sounded as distant and exotic as Tiryns, or Knossos, places at the end of the world.

Jason nodded. "Your fame extends far beyond these mountains."

My guardian said nothing. He disliked flattery. Jason went on, "I would like to buy one of your bows. I have heard that they are perfect."

This was an unfortunate statement, for Castor had strong opinions about perfection. He said it was hard to find and harder to achieve, but hardest of all to forget.

"I have no bows to sell, perfect or otherwise," he told Jason brusquely. "You have made your long trip in vain."

"Truly?" Jason did not raise his voice, but it rang with incredulity. Castor shrugged, as if unaware that half a dozen bows, some newly made, others close to completion, hung from the trees in plain view.

Another man would have argued or pleaded, but Jason did neither. He simply settled near the fire and watched Castor, who turned his attention back to the morning's

29

task, heating and bending two long pieces of ash. Gently, slowly, he persuaded the wood to curve.

I was less successful at ignoring the stranger. As I stirred the glue until it was smoother than honey, I kept wondering what he would do. He had the air of someone who was accustomed to having his way.

After a long while he said, "Chiron is my teacher. He told me the only thing that could save my shooting was one of your bows." Chiron the Centaur was a great archer, admired for his wisdom and sobriety as well as his marksmanship. Later I learned that he had raised Jason from infancy, just as Castor and the other hunters had raised me.

Castor snorted. "He has no taste for flattery, then."

Jason laughed hard and long. "No."

Finally Castor smiled. "Would you care to try one?" he asked.

Jason jumped to his feet. "Yes, yes," he said, "of course."

"Why not shoot against Atalanta?" said Castor. I looked up, startled. "If you can match her, I will give you a bow."

"She shoots?"

"She does."

Jason could not suppress a laugh, perhaps at the notion that I could handle a weapon, or perhaps at my appearance. I was suddenly very conscious of my dingy chiton, my rough-woven cloak, and my filthy bare feet. It was early spring and the mountain streams were still edged with snow, which made bathing a truly Spartan exercise. I was not terribly clean. But at least I had braided my hair, which was more than I could say for him.

When I returned from my shelter with my bow, Castor was pinning a rabbit skin to the great fir at the edge of the clearing. A few of the children appeared, as if they had smelled a contest, or heard of it on the wind. They were always shooting against one another, of course, and they had seen me practice countless times, but a match with a stranger was an unusual treat. They watched us with the wriggling intensity of young dogs awaiting food.

"Three shots from sixty paces," said Castor, after Jason

had chosen a bow. "Left ear, right ear, head." He measured off the distance and drew a line in the ground with a stick.

I no longer wore my cloak, but only my chiton. Now I fastened my wrist guard. It was a soft, supple thing made of spotted cat, a gift from Castor when I won my first shooting contest.

"It will protect your arm," he had said. I prized it almost as much as my bow.

Jason looked at me. I indicated that he should go first, and he stepped up to Castor's mark. He eyed the target, raised his bow to the sky in a swooping salute, then shot. His first arrow missed the tree altogether. His second came within a finger's breadth of the rabbit's right ear. His third shot, his best, hit the center of the rabbit's head.

He stepped back with a slight nod. I realized he was pleased. Even then, I knew how to keep my face expression-less, but there was a trill of mocking laughter from the children, who had not yet learned to dissemble. Every one of them could shoot as well as Jason.

Castor's frown silenced them. Before their laughter had died away, I had taken my three shots. The arrows formed a neat little pattern on the white fur, like an upside-down arrowhead.

"Left ear, right ear, head," I said.

Jason stared at the target open-mouthed.

"Atalanta wins," said Castor.

The young ones whooped and waved their arms, grinning rudely at Jason. Castor chased them off.

I expected Jason to show anger or shame; they were the customary reactions when I won. Instead, he turned my way, lowered his head, and extended an arm to me, palm up. It was an unfamiliar gesture, baffling yet oddly pleasing.

"Your skill is wonderful," he said. His eyes were gray-green, like dark water.

I shrugged, blushing ferociously. "Castor taught me."

"I also had a fine teacher, but instruction can only do so much, as I have just proved." He said this with such a wry smile that I could not help smiling back.

"Atalanta shoots better than I will ever hope to," he said to Castor.

Castor nodded in agreement.

Once again, Jason's smile was wry. He was wonderfully adept at refusing to take offense. "Though I have lost," he said to Castor, "I am loath to leave empty-handed. Will you not relent and sell me a bow?"

"What do you think?" Castor surprised us all by asking me. I looked into Jason's eyes.

"I think he will treat it well," I said.

We were friends from that day.

FIVE

Now I crouched outside Oeneus' palace, forgotten by everyone but Jason, who found me at dusk. At first I could not even look at him, or speak; I was encased in misery, as if Medusa's scowl had turned me to stone. Jason wrapped me in his cloak and offered me some wine. I gulped it down, choking a little; then I cried. I hated the sound of it—*so weak and girlish!*—yet I could not stop myself.

He sat with me for a long time. As the moon rose, he told me the story of Meleager and the Fates.

"They appeared to Queen Althea when Meleager was born," he said, "and she asked them how long he would live.

"As long as it takes for that stick of wood to burn away," said one, pointing to the fire.

"Althea was horrified. The instant they were gone she pulled the stick from the flames and hid it away. Time passed; she watched Meleager grow into a fine young man. The Fates were outwitted, or so she thought."

I had last seen Althea as we departed for the hunt. She had wished me well, putting her small, bejeweled hand on my shoulder, reaching up to press her cheek against mine. She had beautiful dark eyes like her son, and the affection in them had touched my heart. I had thought enviously that Meleager was lucky to have such a mother.

"She learned otherwise, and most cruelly," said Jason.

I tried to imagine Althea's anguish when the Fates told her how soon her child would die. In attempting to save him, she had done what any mother would, yet how could she hope to outwit the Implacable Ones? No mortal has that power.

The Fates simply lay in wait, anticipating the bloody clash between Meleager and his uncles. When it came, it transformed Althea from a protective mother into a murderous one, who killed her son to avenge her brothers.

It was a sequence of events horrible beyond imagining.

"She burned the stick?" I asked.

Jason breathed out heavily. "And then took her own life."

I closed my eyes. I should not have come, I thought. I should have sent an excuse to Meleager and stayed in Arcadia. If I had done so, only the boar would have died. The others would still be alive.

As if he had heard me, Jason said, "Do not blame yourself for any of this."

"How can I not?" I replied, "Even you would not have me on the *Argo*." Fearing that he could not keep peace with a woman aboard, Jason had not invited me on the voyage to Colchis. I had failed to understand his reasoning at the time; I could think only of the glory he and his men had won. From the moment they presented the Golden Fleece to Jason's uncle, King Pelias—to his astonishment, for the

Fleece was guarded by an insomniac serpent with a deadly temper—Jason and his comrades had become demi-gods.

Knowing this had made me all the more eager to join the Hunt, and when Meleager sent word, I had literally raced all the way to Calydon, making the four-day journey in two and a half. Nothing could keep me away; I burned to prove that I belonged in the company of heroes. Even if the boar were Artemis' creature, I told myself, the goddess would understand my need.

I had offered to her liberally before leaving.

But what had I won in Calydon? Terrible sadness for the deaths I had witnessed. Disgrace for the ones I had caused. A name that would be uttered with pity, or worse, linked as it was to the woes of this blighted kingdom. And shame for my kin, who had taken such pride in me.

It was difficult to speak. When at length I could, I asked Jason, haltingly, what I should do.

"Go to Gortys," he said.

SIX

I left the palace before dawn, carrying only my weapons. Aura, Meleager's favorite hound, followed me out. I saw no reason to discourage her. She was a rangy, sociable dog, with a mouse-brown coat, bright amber eyes, and a perpetually wagging tail. Now that Meleager was gone, she would need company.

So would I. Gortys was many days' journey from Calydon, and though I was armed, and could outrun anyone on two legs, Aura would surely be helpful; bandits, as well as centaurs, roamed the hills.

As we approached the gates, she darted ahead of me, neck extended, tail rigid. In the half-light I recognized the boar's head and hide lying near one of the stone pillars.

Aura nosed the malodorous heap eagerly; it was not easy to pull her away.

I wondered if the great trophies of the hunt would be left here to rot, or if they would be fed to the funeral pyres later in the day. Costly offerings, I thought.

The cypresses guarding the palace stood black against an electrum sky. A damp wind promised rain. We took the eastward track downhill. Aura bounded ahead, following her nose. Every now and then she would turn to hurry me on, barking and swinging her tail. I jogged, allowing her to lead, and we went quickly.

At midmorning we stopped at a stream. Clouds of mist hung in the pines. The forest floor was slick with their needles. Here and there, clumps of white cyclamen, Artemis' flower, gleamed like fragments of the moon.

Satisfied that we were well and truly alone, I bathed in the icy water. Once cleansed, I prayed silently to the goddess, dedicating my journey to her and asking for her blessing. "I am yours," I whispered, as I always did. Then Aura ate a squirrel and we moved on.

Even in Arcadia we knew of the oracle at Gortys, which was dedicated to Asclepius. Like his father, Apollo, Asclepius was a great healer who could mend broken minds as well as broken bodies. Supplicants to his oracle slept in caves, hoping to receive their cures in dreams.

Some went for relief, others for answers. Jason had visited the oracle in secret before embarking on his quest. "I dreamed of the Fleece," he told me, "and of a beautiful, bewitching woman. With two such omens, I came away happy." In Colchis he had met the woman in his dream, a princess called Medea. She had used powerful magic to help him, and later become his wife.

I had also heard tales of miracles at Gortys, of the blind regaining their sight, of the palsied rising up and bounding away, and of barren women (it was one of the few oracles where women were permitted) becoming fruitful within days. I cherished the story of a mute boy who regained his speech after dreaming of silver-tongued Apollo.

I wondered if I, too, might dream of Apollo, for I had spoken little since the Hunt, responding even to Jason with grinding effort. It was as if I were a child again, overhearing the hunters' talk of what my father had done. *Left her to die. Didn't want a girl.* The words, flatly spoken, had so transfixed and bewildered me that I had been mute for days.

Now, too, I felt wrapped in silence, as if my grief were a heavy, stifling garment I could not shed. I ran on, ignoring my pangs of hunger. I had not eaten since the Hunt, and would not until I reached Gortys.

In this small way I thought to honor Meleager's death.

SEVEN

Early the next morning we waited at the shore for the boat-
man, an old fellow as gnarled and squat as a tree stump. He
had ferried me across this same deep channel only ten
days before, with Ancaeus and Cepheus. Their loud conversation with him had not ceased for all the time of
crossing.

Today it was different.

Seeing me alone, he was full of questions. I made him
understand with gestures that Ancaeus and Cepheus were
gone. It may have been this grim news, or the flash of
Aura's teeth when she bared them, but he left us in peace
after that. When at last we reached the far shore, I gave
him two small game birds in payment; one was for his
silence.

A vast, sandy plain stretched before us. Mountains loomed to the north, with Gortys in the foothills, two days' walk from here, and two more from home.

We had much distance to cover, and again Aura set the pace, bounding ahead as if released from a trap. We were soon loping along in unison, enjoying the windy salt air, with its fish-bone-and-seaweed perfume.

When they saw us approaching, groups of children would run down to meet us, and Aura would circle them, prancing and wagging her tail. They would often try to race us, screaming with excitement when I let them catch up, and shouting in surprise when I shot ahead. At such times Aura would bark sharply, joyously. Like me, she was happiest in the lead.

After a time I knew only the steady slap of my feet and the pounding of my heart. The waves beat nearby like a soft, insistent drum, and my mind eased, then stilled altogether. I was in motion, but I might have been sitting under a tree, dissolving into the breath of the forest.

I ran on, as if I were passing a shadowy crowd of straining opponents, one by one by one.

The sky went from crimson to indigo. The moon rose, veiled in drifts like cobwebs. Lights—torches—flickered in the distance. Hearing chanting, I stopped.

We had reached the oracle.

EIGHT

Apollo: She's fast!

Artemis: Chaste, too. And devoted.

Apollo: Then why are you making her suffer?

Artemis: I didn't mean to. It was bad planning.

Apollo: Shall I send her a good dream?

Artemis: I was hoping I could count on you.

The cave was small, and low enough to make me stoop, but the straw pallet was laid with a cloud of fluffy white rams' skins, and a rough drawing of Asclepius the Healer, complete with snake-entwined staff, hovered reassuringly on the wall.

The silence inside was complete. With the sound of my own heartbeat sounding in my ears, I looked around in the torchlight, overwhelmed by the sense that I had been here before. No harm will come to me in this place, I thought, as the cave embraced me in some powerful yet long-forgotten fashion. With the thought my bones fairly melted, and I dropped to my knees in exhaustion.

Aura settled herself near the entrance, and the attendant who had greeted us and led us here—her name, she said, was Zoi—hobbled out. A moment later she returned with a small terra-cotta cup.

"Drink after you pray," she said. Her eyes, a clear, innocent blue, met mine for the first time. "Heed well what you dream." She gave me the cup.

When I was alone, I asked Asclepius to heal my heart-sickness. I asked Artemis to guide me with a firm hand. I asked Zeus, Lord of all Creation, to smile on Meleager's shade and grant it peace.

The dark liquid smelled like wood tar. It was terribly bitter, but I drank it all. Then I slept.

* * *

I am in a shadowy, high-ceilinged room. A man sits before me, wrapped in a cloak. His face is waxen, his eyes red-rimmed, and he is gaunt enough to be mortally ill.

There are three golden bowls on the floor before his throne, brimming with bloody organs and entrails. From their size I guess they are animal rather than human, and wonder if they are offerings.

The man beckons, and the heavy gold rings on his long fingers clack like bones. I do not wish to show fear, but I hesitate. Seeing this, he grins hugely.

Artemis and I are in a pine grove, reclining together in the manner of old friends. Her great hound, Phoebus, lounges nearby with Aura. The air is soft and fragrant and I am completely at ease with the goddess, as if she and I often passed time together this way.

I feel I can ask her anything. "I have been wondering what to do now that the Hunt is over," I say.

"Whatever you do," she replies, lifting her fine eyebrows

48

ever so slightly for emphasis, "avoid marriage." Her eyes, catching mine, are a pale gray-green, the color of lichen.

"Marriage will bring you trouble," she adds.

I have very little interest in marriage. "More trouble!" I exclaim lightly. "Is that possible?"

She laughs, revealing a tiny gap between her two front teeth. "Anything is possible," she says mischievously, "but surely you knew that?"

Now I do, I think. I repeat her words silently, and they warm my heart: *anything is possible.*

I am running along the ocean. The sand is as fine and as white as linen, welcoming me with every stride. I hear the deep thrum of footsteps behind me and know that I am in a race. My legs have never felt stronger; I might be wearing winged sandals like Hermes, messenger of the gods. I pick up the pace without effort and pull far ahead of my opponents, breathing deeply and easily, enjoying the absolute certainty that I will win.

* * *

I am lying in a thicket of brambles, curled around a small, warm body that nuzzles me, mewling. My eyes are closed. I am exhausted, yet so wonderfully content that I fairly vibrate with happiness. I find the body—so tiny next to mine—and lick it again and again and again.

NINE

I woke slowly, to the warm, wet touch of Aura's tongue on my face. From her insistence, and her expression of concern, I guessed that she had been trying to rouse me for some time. I patted her silky head, wondering how long I had slept, then stumbled outside. The sky was the powdery blue of a jay's crest, the sun directly overhead. No wonder Aura had been anxious. The day was half gone.

I stretched, yawning, and as I stood there with my arms flung wide, my dreams came back to me, one by one— bright, tremulous, and clear as rocks in a mountain stream. Startled, I sank to my knees.

Four dreams, I thought. Four messages.

I settled on the ground cross-legged and closed my eyes.

They came to me without effort, and I admired each one

51

as I might admire an exotic flower, or a finely wrought javelin. They were beautiful. Even the first, so fraught with menace, gleamed alluringly. The rings sparkled; the organs in the golden bowls shimmered like jewels.

I vowed to remember them always, for I knew they were precious even if their meaning was obscure. They had been sent; that was enough, and I was grateful. My understanding would come in time. For now I felt forgiven—though for what I could not tell—and blessed.

My eyes filled, and I heaved such a gusty sigh of relief that Aura rushed over to me, whining. She barked, eyes aglow, then cocked her ears at the sound of my rumbling stomach.

I sprang to my feet. "Let's eat," I said.

Artemis: Well done, brother. Thank you.
Apollo: You are welcome. I do enjoy doing prophetic dreams.

Artemis: These were lovely, though you may have revealed too much with that last one. The fur, the licking—?

Apollo: Great thundering Zeus! She's happy now, isn't she? She's talking again, isn't she? I thought you wanted to help her!

Artemis: All right, all right. Forget I said anything. The dreams are wonderful. And they will help her—in ways that I never could.

Apollo: Is that an apology?

Artemis: Older sisters don't apologize. You know that.

When I met Zoi on the path to the beach, she greeted me by saying quietly, "Your prayers have been heard."

Smiling, I replied, "I am fortunate." The hunters had told me this so often—usually when I was howling with outrage at some terrible childhood injustice—that it felt odd to be saying the words with such conviction, to know beyond a doubt that they were true.

She tilted her head appraisingly. Her hair was as white as sea-foam, her face as lined and weathered as driftwood.

"You are hungry?"

I laughed. "So hungry."

"Come." She led us down to her tiny, whitewashed hut. Next to it, sheltered by tall pines, was a shrine, and a painted wooden statue of Asclepius. Dappled sunlight played across the god's face, which wore a placid smile.

Zoi brought bread, honey, dried fish, figs, grapes, and a jug of lemon water. I placed an offering of food on the shrine, bowing. Then Aura and I consumed every remaining morsel.

When we finished, I thanked Zoi, adding, "I am Atalanta. From Arcadia."

"The huntress."

I must have looked surprised that she knew.

"You arrived with a hound, carrying a bow," she said dryly, adding, "I also have been sent dreams. One of them was about you."

54

I waited.

"You stood before Artemis and Aphrodite," she said. "They asked you to choose between them. You chose Artemis."

So I would, I thought. My loyalty had always been to Artemis, Mistress of the Wild. Aphrodite, who busied herself ensnaring lovers, seemed soft and foolish by comparison.

At my nod Zoi said, "The decision brought you pain. A wound . . ." She faltered, her eyelids fluttering like moths.

"A wound?" The words filled me with alarm. I had never been injured, and feared the experience mightily, though I kept that to myself.

"Sudden. Very deep. That is all I know." She placed a small brown hand on mine. It was as light and dry as a withered leaf.

"Your fame as a hunter will grow," she said, patting me. "Poets down the years will sing of Atalanta's strength, her wild spirit, her beauty. The splendor of your legend will far outlive you."

Joy and bewilderment made me flush. If Zoi's words were true, I would have all the glory I had ever yearned for. Yet how could she know my future?

"How—?" I began. Ignoring me, she pulled herself to her feet. I rose hastily. "Please tell me," I asked her, "did you dream that also?"

The smile on her face was as enigmatic as the statue's.

"Safe journey home," she said.

PART TWO

The Homecoming

They entered our settlement on horses, frightening everyone. The children recovered first, hurtling back into the
clearing as if they were running one of their wild races.
Were these giant four-legged creatures cousins of the
winged horse, Pegasus? Were they strays from Lord
Poseidon's savage herd? Chittering with excitement, the
children came as close to the horses as they dared, while the
women, who had probably mistaken the mounted strangers
for centaurs, emerged from the trees slowly, whispering im-
precations.

The men of the tribe were out hunting. Only the two
eldest, our headman, Bias, and Castor, had remained behind. Just as he had taught me to make traps before I could
speak, Castor had taught me to feather arrows, and when

the riders appeared, I had been helping him. I liked the work, which required no thought, only a light touch. It gave me good reason to sit with Castor—the least garrulous of men—in prolonged, uneventful silence. Since my return home some days before, I had wanted little else.

Now I felt a long thrill of amazement. Men rode to battle in horse-drawn chariots—I knew this because Jason had told me—but I had never seen them sitting astride before. It was a wondrous sight.

After surprise came a less familiar sensation: the slow, insistent burn of wanting and not having. Who were these men, looking down at us with such arrogance? How had they come to handle these magnificent creatures with such ease? I hated them.

Bias greeted them calmly, as if the appearance of men on large walnut-brown steeds were an everyday occurrence. The gleaming horses stood motionless as he approached, and when Aura wove between their tall, finely chiseled legs, sniffing eagerly, they did not even flick their tails; it was as if she were beneath their notice.

"We come on behalf of King Iasus," said the older of the two, a broad-faced, balding, curly-bearded man. "He sends for his daughter."

The king lived in a region of Arcadia far below our own. Of him, I knew only that he was growing old, had once been fond of hunting, and lacked an heir. I had heard no mention of a daughter.

Beside me, Castor grunted softly, as if hit in the belly by a rock. Bias' head dropped, and for a moment he said nothing. Then he asked, "He . . . wants her now?"

The men nodded. They wore leather sandals and deep blue chitons. The handles of their short swords were inlaid with colored stones. The older man looked around the clearing somewhat impatiently.

"Prove you come from the king." Castor said this abruptly, rising to join Bias. The older rider drew in his chin and raised an eyebrow. Surely, his expression said, our splendid horses and imposing weapons are proof enough!

"We must know she will be safe with you," added Castor, by way of explanation.

The men looked at each other, then dismounted. The younger man stroked Aura's head, which set her tail to sweeping the ground like a maddened snake. The older man produced a small leather pouch, reached inside, and showed something to Castor and Bias. There was a bright golden flash as they passed it between them.

Bias turned my way. His expression was both stern and regretful, as if he were about to deliver judgment, or mete out punishment. I have done nothing wrong! I thought, as dread grabbed me by the throat. Suddenly I felt very young.

"Atalanta," he said, "come look at this."

It was a gold ring, heavy enough to stun a crow. Carved into it was a double thunderbolt, the weapon of Almighty Zeus. The man who wore this had a very high opinion of himself, I thought, rolling it in my palm, and wondering where I had seen such a thing before.

"It is the king's," said Castor, and Bias nodded slowly, almost unwillingly.

The king's, I thought, for suddenly I could not speak.

"Atalanta." Bias said my name with such sadness and finality that I quivered. Wanting suddenly to be rid of the ring, but knowing my impulse came too late, I gave it back to him. Now the children were silent, and I heard broken whispers from the women.

A preternatural stillness came over me, and I thought of the Fates—patient, inescapable. It was as if, by touching the ring, I had agreed to something that had been decided long, long ago.

Aware that the horsemen were watching me, I straightened, standing tall. Then they stepped forward, claiming me for my father.

ELEVEN

I gathered my few belongings and made my farewells.

"Remember us," said Castor, and my mouth trembled. Feeling the press of his warm, sure hand on my head, I whispered that I would see him soon, for to say anything else would have made me cry.

Then we set off down the mountain. The men, who had introduced themselves curtly as Mataios and Perifanos, led their horses down the steep, rocky trails in silence. From time to time the horses slid, and the men exchanged uneasy glances. They might have done better fetching me on mountain goats, I thought spitefully.

Before long, Aura and I forgot ourselves and went too far ahead of them. The first time we were lost to their view, I heard Mataios—the elder—call out, "Princess!"

I stopped in my tracks.

Princess! I thought, jarred by the sound of it. As we waited there, I wondered if Meleager's uncle Plexippus, who had called me a slut with dirt between her toes (and he was right about the dirt), might have curbed his rage if he had known I was royalty. Perhaps. Most certainly he would still be alive.

I scowled, disliking the memory and where it led. My visit to the oracle had eased my mind about the Hunt and its terrible consequences, and I could think of them now with some measure of calm. Still, I did not like to think of them at all.

Then, as I stood there, the first of my oracle dreams came back to me.

The skeletal man beckoned, and I knew that he was King Iasus, the father who had left me to die when I was born. I knew also that he was weak, nearly moribund, yet possessed of a strong malevolence. My fear of the bloody bowls at his feet gave him great satisfaction.

I wondered if the king intended to harm me, and if the entrails were indeed human. Everyone knew that human sacrifice was still practiced in some parts of Arcadia. Was the king inviting me to sacrifice myself?

I shivered. And where was the queen? Nowhere in the dream, I thought. Absent, just as she had been absent from my life.

With this thought the men reached us. They were panting, and their horses were blowing a little. Dark patches of sweat marked their coats.

"The paths up here are difficult," I observed.

Mataios caught his breath. "You do not seem to find them so," he said.

"I know them well," I replied.

"Are we far from the field with the shepherd's hut?" he asked.

"No, it is—" I was interrupted by a high-pitched, wavering call, like an eerie scream. It was not the call of any bird I knew.

66

The horses' ears shot forward and a low, ruffling sound came from deep within their throats. Perifanos' horse backed a little, tossing his head. Then he, too, cried out shrilly, and from a distance the call came back.

"There they are," said Mataios with evident relief.

"More horses?" I asked.

"One more," said Perifanos, and now he was smiling. "For you."

Her name was Callisto. She was dainty and copper-colored, adorned with tassels, and when she saw us, she whinnied again, swishing her tail. Her eyes and lashes were dark, and her flaring nostrils were pink, like the inside of a shell. She was beautiful.

The boy at her side patted her neck soothingly.

"Is she named for the nymph?" I asked. Callisto, a lovely wood nymph, was pursued by Lord Zeus and bore him a son. Hoping to protect her from his wife Hera's jealousy, Zeus changed the nymph into a bear. Hera promptly sent

Artemis on a bear hunt, so Zeus vaulted Callisto into the heavens. Now a bear made of stars, she floats in the night sky.

Perifanos had jumped off his horse. As it munched the sparse greenery, he nodded. I was pleased. The appearance of a horse with a bear's name seemed like a good omen. Any reminder that Artemis had sent a bear to save my life gladdened me, and now my spirits rose a little.

"Callisto," I said, and her ear flicked back, then forward. To my delight, she licked my hand when I held it out to her.

Perifanos, who leaned against his horse, smiled.

"We should be going," Mataios said. "We have a long ride. Koris, help the princess up," he added brusquely.

As Koris came around to me, I watched to see how Perifanos mounted. He stood at his horse's side with his hands placed lightly on its back, then jumped, swinging his right leg up and over. Then he was astride, reins in hand, as if the wind god Zephyrus had blown him there on the gentlest of breezes. The feat seemed effortless, but I knew it was not. Every muscle in Perifanos' back had flexed when he rose.

Standing next to me at Callisto's side, Koris pointed to my left foot, then cupped his big, rough hands and offered them to me encouragingly. I felt a stab of panic. I could shoot and I could run. But could I mount a horse without immodesty? Conscious that the men were watching, I arranged my chiton so that it would not open when I jumped. Then I stepped into Koris' hands and hoisted myself up as if I were climbing a tree. I swung my leg as Perifanos had, and lowered myself gently onto Callisto's back. My chiton remained closed through all of this, a small miracle.

Callisto's warm sides felt good against my calves. I looked over at Perifanos to see how he was holding his reins and quickly arranged mine the same way.

"The princess is ready," said Mataios. It was less a question than a gruff acknowledgment.

I sat up a little straighter. "I am," I said, wishing it were true.

TWELVE

Many hours later, as we came within sight of the palace, the horses tossed their heads and began to jig. Then, as if at a signal, they took the long, uphill slope at a breakneck run. Callisto had been lagging behind. Now she bolted ahead as if stung by a gadfly, and I found myself slipping off her back. I grabbed desperately at her mane, but it did no good. Unless she slowed down, which was clearly not her intention, I would fall.

The ground was very stony.

All afternoon I had marveled at our horses' speed, at the way their long legs devoured the roads and fields almost magically. In my admiration they had become noble beings, almost worthy of reverence.

Now, as they bolted, my infatuation ended. With my legs

flopping and my arms flailing, I could think only one bitter thought: thanks to a horse, I was about to suffer grievous public humiliation.

"Lean forward," called Perifanos. He was taking the hill in a kind of half-crouch, and when I somehow managed to imitate him, my balance improved at once.

"Thank you," I gasped. Then, to shouted greetings from the walls, we slowed.

A pair of massive bronze doors opened, and we trotted into a spacious courtyard. A boy who might have been Koris' brother helped me off Callisto, for which I was grateful—my legs were as limp as empty sacks—and led her away. After a moment Aura appeared, wagging her tail, none the worse for wear. An elderly pair of hounds sauntered over to sniff her. Ever mannerly, she bowed in greeting.

Mataios and Perifanos took their leave.

For a moment I was alone, standing unsteadily before a large stucco building with handsome wooden doors and many windows. I wondered how it could possibly be my father's home, for it was nothing like the shadowy, gloom-ridden place of my dream, where malice hung in the air like torch smoke. Everything here bespoke prosperity and order.

A woman with pale speckled skin, small and round as a hen, bustled over to me. "Greetings, lady," she said amiably, looking me up and down as if trying to decide which part of me to clean first. "I am Entella. I will show you your quarters."

The floor inside, white stone streaked with gray, was wonderfully cool beneath my grimy feet. Aura's nails clacked as she walked sedately at my side. I marveled at her perfect composure until I remembered that she had once belonged to a prince. She had spent far more time in palaces than I ever had.

"Where is the king?" I asked.

"He is resting," said Entella, indicating a hallway to our left. "He will meet you at dusk." I followed her past a large, high-ceilinged central chamber, where rows of benches squatted before a single throne. Only one throne, I thought, following Entella down another long hallway to the right. Why is that?

We came to the end and she opened a door.

"Here we are," she said, leading me into a large, sunlit room. I looked around warily. Though it was well furnished, the room had an air of neglect about it, as if it had lain empty for years. The skin of a huge striped animal sprawled across the floor, its mouth frozen in a snarl, its glass eyes staring. Two heavy spears, crossed above the massive bull-hide shield on the wall, looked as if they had not been used since Zeus battled Cronus at the dawn of time. A low table with gold claw legs sat next to the carved bed; on the table were a silver water pitcher and cup. It was all very princely, and nothing like my deerskin shelter in the forest, which—along with Castor, and Bias—I suddenly missed very much.

I set down my bow and quiver, barely suppressing a groan, for now I ached fiercely from ribs to knees. My seat and the backs of my thighs burned as if they had been flayed, and I wondered with alarm if riding a horse always caused such misery. That would be dire. Despite my near-calamitous arrival, I very much wanted to ride again.

I will, I told myself, if I recover. When I recover.

"Will you bathe, my lady?" asked Entella. "Or would you prefer to rest?"

"I will bathe," I said, which seemed to please her. On the way to the women's bath, she told me she would be serving me, and laughed when I asked her what that meant.

"I will try to keep you clean and well fed," she said.

"Will you feed Aura also?" I asked.

"If you keep her clean."

"Done."

"If you let me, I will arrange your hair and help you dress."

"I will," I said. I liked her forthrightness. She could have been one of my tribe.

"Then I will come to you later, to prepare you for the evening," she said.

I expected blisters or worse when I undressed, but found only a few bruises and some chafed skin. Not so bad, I told myself, settling into the bath with a heartfelt groan of relief. Not so bad at all.

I sank, then rose to the surface so that only my face was above water. While I floated there, a startling, hopeful thought came to me: what if my dream of the king was not a portent, but a divine joke? What if the gods, for sport, had tricked me into fearing him?

"Perhaps he is a good, kind, loving man," I murmured dreamily. "Anything is possible. Artemis herself told me so."

Artemis: Poor thing.

Apollo: Save your pity. She doesn't need it.

Artemis: How do you know?

Apollo: I'm oracular, remember?

Artemis: That doesn't mean you're infallible.

Apollo: I'll wager she can handle him.

Artemis: How much?

Apollo: Two of my best arrows.

Artemis: Three—the ivory ones, that Hephaestus made.

Apollo: Agreed. If I win, I'll take your ivory quiver.

Artemis: That's my favorite!

Apollo: I know.

THIRTEEN

Entella came at sunset with a finely woven white chiton, which she fastened at my shoulder with a gold pin. Then she sat me down and combed and braided my hair, rolling my head this way and that as if it were a melon. Her plump, dexterous hands smelled of rosemary.

When I was groomed to her satisfaction, she escorted me into the courtyard. "Wait here," she said. "He will be coming soon."

I sat on a stone bench and watched the light seep out of the sky. The cicadas began their loud, tuneless song. At length I heard a door open and the murmur of voices. Someone called my name. I rose, my palms so wet they left dark imprints on the stone. Then, taking a deep breath, I crossed the courtyard.

He was very tall, handsome despite his gauntness, with dark, watchful eyes and a black beard streaked white. Thick black eyebrows crossed his forehead in an emphatic line, giving him the look of someone who was difficult to please.

There was no denying the resemblance between us. My eyes and hair were brown, not black, but our foreheads were the same, high and domed, and then there was my height. I was nearly as tall as he was.

He is your father, I told myself, like it or not.

He stepped forward with the help of a wooden staff, and the small, plump, fair-haired woman beside him gave me a quick, timorous smile. She could not be my mother, I thought—she was too young, and looked nothing like me at all. Her dress and jewels were of such richness that she could not be a servant, either.

"Welcome, daughter," said my father. His voice was unexpectedly deep and soft, like a caress.

"Father." I, too, stepped forward, revealing myself in the torchlight.

78

His mouth twisted in a spasm of pain, or strong emotion. Then he scrutinized me so slowly and carefully that I might have been goods for barter. I stood there until he beckoned me closer, the gold rings on his long fingers chiming.

There is something strangely familiar about this, I thought, walking into his awkward, one-armed embrace—he was all bones—and then my dream came back to me.

I pulled away.

He looked startled, but the fair-haired woman smiled again, as if everything about our meeting was just as it should be. She rose on tiptoe, whispering loudly into my father's ear, "Iasus, will you introduce me?"

"This is Nephele," he said flatly, without looking at her. "My wife."

But where is my mother? I longed to ask, knowing I could not. Instead, I bowed my head.

"Welcome," said Nephele, returning the gesture. "We have heard much of you." Taking hold of my father's elbow, she began to lead him into the palace.

"And many stirring accounts of the Hunt in Calydon," added my father. He moved very slowly. "It is said that you were more agile than Theseus, more daring than Jason, and so much stronger than Hercules that he fled in shame."

I laughed. "Hercules did not even attend," I said.

"Really?" He seemed disappointed. "And the other great heroes—Theseus and Jason?"

I pictured Jason, reunited with his kin in distant Thessaly. For all he knew, I was at home also, much recovered after journeying to Gortys. I wondered what he would say if he could see me. No doubt he would be astonished. Then, being Jason, he would recover quickly, and make some nimble jest about my sudden elevation to nobility. I wished he were close by; he alone could make me laugh at this.

"Jason attended," I said. "Theseus also."

"Is it true that you wrestled the boar in a swamp and then strangled it with your bare hands?" asked Nephele.

"I wish I had," I replied. "It would have prevented a great deal of suffering." At this my father looked at me sharply.

Had he been anticipating a breathless paean to the glories of the Hunt? If so, he was about to be disappointed.

We came to a small, square chamber, its pale yellow walls painted with leaping bucks and flying arrows. Nephele helped my father to sit. Once in his chair, he called for wine.

An old man scuttled in as if he had been poised for the summons, filling my father's silver goblet to the brim. Nephele waved him away, as I did. Where I came from, we drank wine only when sacrificing; even then I was not overly fond of it.

My father drained his goblet hastily, as if taking a potion. Then, seemingly surprised to find the goblet empty, he motioned for more. The old man refilled it, and again my father drank.

Food was set before us—olives, bread, lentils, roast mutton. Nephele began to eat without delay, murmuring appreciatively. The food was rich in oil and spices. It tasted wonderful.

My father did not even look at it. "We heard that you wrestled the mighty Peleus and won."

This was the most outlandish thing I had ever heard. Wrestlers competed naked; surely my father knew that.

"I did not," I said. "Nor would I. Ever."

The dark eyebrows went up.

"I am chaste, and a devotee of Artemis," I informed him. "I would never appear unclothed in public."

"Artemis?" he said, raising an eyebrow. The manner in which he said this one word made me feel as if I were an ignorant child.

Before I could reply, Nephele said hastily, "We—we have heard so much praise of you, so many glowing reports. It is hard to know what is true and what is not."

"Be assured that I did not wrestle Peleus," I said.

"You did attend the Hunt, did you not?" inquired my father. "Or is that yet another wild fable?"

"I was there."

"So," he said, as if the admission were a minor victory for him, "tell us what you did."

"Please," said Nephele. "We are so eager to hear of it—from you."

"I was the only woman, and the only hunter with a bow."

At this, my father's mouth twitched downward in something like approbation.

"I drew first blood," I added.

"Were you awarded?" he asked quickly.

"Meleager gave me the trophies," I said, "but—"

"Oeneus' son? Gave you the head and hide?"

I nodded. He motioned for more wine, exclaiming, "The head and hide of the great Calydonian Boar! Well done! I will hang them in the throne room!" His voice rang with delight.

When I said nothing, but only toyed with my food, he thought to ask, "Where are they? The trophies?"

"I do not have them," I said.

He frowned. "Were they stolen?"

"I left them in Calydon."

This drew a look of pure astonishment. "Why?"

I hesitated, knowing my answer would displease him. "They came at too great a price."

"Too great a price," he echoed softly. "Too great a price! I know men who would have died for those trophies."

I glared at him. "I know men who did," I said.

"Oh!" Nephele gasped. "How terrible!"

"It was," I said, remembering Meleager's death agony.

"Terrible or not," said my father, waving his hand dismissively, "you achieved no small fame in Calydon."

"I was not aware," I retorted.

Bursts of pink appeared on his face, and his brows came together in a thick, dark line. "How could you be aware of anything," he asked, his sonorous voice suddenly tinged with venom, "hiding in the mountains with those miserable bark-eaters?"

He is drunk, I thought, feeling both dread and anger.

He gave me a joyless smile. "Things will be different now," he said. "You are a princess. You belong here, in the palace, not roaming the forests." He drank. "And there is your duty to consider."

"My duty?"

"I lack an heir."

I did not understand what one had to do with the other. Nor did I understand how he and Nephele could be childless. She seemed healthy enough to bear an army of children.

I turned to her. Eyes downcast, face expressionless, she shook her head.

"One was stillborn," said my father, as if he were talking about livestock. "Then she miscarried. The last one died young."

"Two months." It was a whispered lament.

My father was unmoved. "You are my only offspring," he

said to me, "and my health is failing." He drained his goblet and set it down unsteadily. It wobbled and fell, surrendering a few brown dregs to the table.

"So I have decided to marry you off. Word has gone out to other royal houses of the region, those with eligible sons. Many have responded. It appears you will have a choice of consorts," he added, as if delivering good tidings.

"You will select one quickly, and produce a son without delay. He—my grandson—will inherit the throne."

FOURTEEN

I felt as cold and vaporous as a shade, as if I were hovering outside myself, watching to see what the girl at the table would do.

I saw her raising her arms to Artemis in a frenzied plea for help.

I saw her loose an arrow that pierced the king's brittle chest, drawing blood and yellow bile.

I saw her flee with her hound into the deepest recesses of Arcadia, as if pursued by the Furies.

Then the moment passed, and I was sitting there dully, stunned into silence by my father's pronouncement.

"Help me up," he ordered Nephele. She gave me a sad, surreptitious smile before leading him away.

Eventually I returned to my chamber and sat down

heavily on the bed. Aura joined me, and I stroked her mouse-colored coat. When she lay down, making little noises of contentment, I settled beside her and recalled my dream of the goddess. Once again, she told me to avoid marriage. Once again, I understood that despite her playful manner, she meant me to obey her, and I resolved to do just that.

But my father was commanding me to marry.

My eyes flew open, and I felt the raw terror of a rabbit in a snare. I told myself that Artemis would help me, that she would send me a dream, and the terror subsided.

As I had done at Gortys, I knelt and prayed for her guidance. Then, becalmed, I slept.

The sky was still dark when I woke. I searched my mind for some sign from the goddess, but all I saw was a riderless horse, head bowed, on its way to the palace. It was a melancholy image I did not understand.

Castor had once told me to think of disappointment as rain or fog, weather of the mind that would inevitably pass.

I was ten years old and not yet allowed to hunt with the men, though I could shoot as well as any of them, and out-run them, too. I had cried bitter tears, taking little comfort from his words, yet I had never forgotten them. Now they gave me a kind of bleak solace.

"I will run," I decided. Stretching cautiously, I found that I was stiff, but no longer aching. It would be good to leave the palace.

My old chiton was on the claw-foot table, folded neatly. It had become very clean—Entella's work, no doubt. "It will not be clean for long," I thought, putting it on.

After I persuaded Aura to leave the bed, we crept through the darkness, passing one snoring guard in the throne room and another in the courtyard. Beyond the dining chamber were more hallways, and rows of store-rooms and kitchens. Then we were outside again, this time at the back of the palace. Two little kitchen maids, curled up near the hearth, stirred as we walked by, but did not waken.

A sliver of moon hung low in the sky, offering the quietest possible greeting. An owl hooted, once.

A few of the horses, tethered to a line under an open shed, raised their heads and nickered. One of them was the lovely Callisto, whose nose was as soft as moss when I stroked it.

"We will ride again soon," I told her, and her ears came forward.

By now Aura and I had drawn the attention of the guards at the wall. The two men flanked a pair of tall wooden doors. Straightening as we drew near, they stared at us with undisguised curiosity before mumbling a greeting.

"Will you let us out?" I asked. Aura did her part by wagging her tail beseechingly.

They exchanged a look. "We cannot, my lady," said one.

"Why not?" I had been free to roam at will since the time I could walk; now I felt a quiver of panic at the threat of confinement.

"We have orders," said the other.

"You are not to leave the palace without an escort."

"Ah." I cocked my head, as if the restriction were entirely reasonable. "I suppose I will have to find one, then."

Turning, I headed back to the palace.

"I cannot carry you!" I hissed from the top of the wall. Years of climbing trees had made it easy to get up here; less easy was convincing Aura that she must stay behind, without barking.

After much entreaty—and promises of tasty bones, long runs, and half the bed—she finally dropped to her haunches with a baleful look. I climbed down the outside face and dropped into the tall grass, quickly finding the track I had ridden on horseback yesterday.

Then I ran.

I went east, feeling a burst of joy to be well outside the walls and in motion. I was glad for the strength in my legs, for the steady beating of my heart, and for the cool embrace of the air as I found my speed and held it. Most welcome of

91

all was the gradual quieting of my mind, the slow fading of inner voices and nagging worries.

My awareness became pure sensation, moving from breath to earth and back again. Then, as if the goddess herself were whispering in my ear, the solution to my dilemma came to me.

I would tell my father that I would marry only if certain conditions were met. If he agreed to them—and I thought he would—no man would ever claim me for his bride. Even as I appeared to honor my father's demands, I would remain true to the goddess. Then I would return home, where I belonged.

Much cheered, I raced the dawn back to the palace, and was in my room before the sky turned pink.

FIFTEEN

Entella was surprised to find me awake when she came to my room at sunup, and highly displeased to find my chiton, the very one she had washed only hours before, sweat-stained and grimy.

"How did you get it so dirty?" she asked.

"I . . . visited the horses."

"The horses?" She said the words almost mournfully, and her plump mouth turned down at the corners, so that she looked like a baby preparing to wail.

"I'm sorry," I said. "I should have tried to keep it clean."

Her eyes filled. Puzzled and alarmed—would she weep every time I dirtied my clothing?—I asked, "What troubles you?"

"Your . . ." She stopped, took a breath, began again. "You

are a princess, not a stable girl," she said. "Now please give me that thing."

I removed it and she hurried out of the room. When she returned with another, of much finer weave, I allowed her to put it on me, and then to fuss with my hair.

"I suppose I will need another garment or two," I said, thinking to make amends.

"You will need many, now that you are here. Jewels, also."

"Jewels?" I could not imagine adorning myself with gold trinkets, though I knew many women liked them. The ladies of Oeneus' court, assembling before the Hunt, had fairly clanked with the stuff—medallions and diadems, armlets and rings and earrings, given them when they bore male children.

"They would only get in my way," I said.

"In your way?" Entella asked.

"When I hunted, or raced."

"But . . . you are a lady of the palace now. Surely—"

"Being here will not stop me from hunting. I will never give that up, no matter where I live," I declared.

Entella's hands grew still. Then she said, "You are like your mother."

"You knew her?" I felt almost dizzy. I had thought of my mother often over the years, with confusion, and yearning, and sometimes bitter curiosity. It was easy to hate my father after learning what he had done, and I had. If last night were any indication, I was welcome to continue; he seemed bent on encouraging my loathing. But my mother was different. She had always been a puzzle, remote yet haunting. All I knew of her was her name, Clymene. I wanted more.

I turned so that I faced Entella. "Tell me about her," I pleaded. "What was she like?"

"Tall, beautiful, restless," Entella said fondly. "She was from Iolcus, in Thessaly, a distant relation of the king."

"Which king? Pelias?" Jason, heir to the throne of Thessaly, had been forced into hiding as a boy when his uncle Pelias seized power. After years in the care of Chiron the

Centaur, he came before Pelias to claim his birthright. Pelias sent him after the Golden Fleece, assuming his nephew would never return alive. It was a serious mistake.

Entella nodded.

"You said I am like her. How?"

"In appearance. In bearing. She was forthright, as you are. And . . . she loved horses."

"Ah. So she was like a stable girl, too?" I asked. The thought warmed me.

Entella nodded. "She told my mother, who served her, that she would rather live with them than in the palace. That shocked my mother so!" Entella's plump face worked with emotion.

"Why?" The words made sense to me, given my father's temperament.

"My mother was terrified of horses," Entella began. ". . . And then, when . . ." She stopped. Her face seemed to crumple.

"What?" I asked.

"Excuse me, my lady," she said, visibly distressed. "I must go."

"Don't leave." Surprised by the hot tears in my eyes, I reached for her hand. "Please," I whispered. "I never knew her. I want to hear more."

"When the king exposed you, the queen begged him to change his mind," she said. "But he refused. She fled the palace on her horse. Many hours later the horse returned alone."

"It was a black horse," I said, "with a white mark on its brow."

Entella's tear-filled eyes widened. "How do you know?"

I saw it again, as I had on waking. "A dream," I said, and then, "Please go on."

"She was in the forest. She had hung herself. My mother said that the queen died of despair when she could not find you."

SIXTEEN

"I will marry, but only if two conditions are met," I told my father when we were seated. Once again, he and Nephele and I were dining. Once again, his meal was wine.

"What are they?"

"First, the man I marry must outrun me."

He laughed in surprise. "So you favor a contest!" he exclaimed. "Well, well. You are my daughter after all."

And my mother's also, I thought.

"What is your second condition?" he asked.

"Anyone who loses against me must die."

Nephele drew in her breath so sharply that she squeaked.

"You are joking," said my father, "aren't you?" His smile was less assured now. There was a brief silence while he waited for me to reassure him. Instead, I shook my head with my eyes narrowed. He must believe I meant every word.

"Well!" he exclaimed, pulling in his chin with a frown. "That is rather harsh. Why should I agree to it? Why would any of your suitors agree to it?"

I had thought carefully of how I would answer.

"As you say, I am your daughter, and your only child. You would not let me go cheaply, would you?" Unspoken between us was the knowledge that he had once thought me utterly worthless, and had thrown me away. If there were the faintest fissure of regret in his rocky heart, I was resolved to hammer at it.

When he did not reply, I continued, "Moreover, if I marry a man who is my equal, your kingdom will reap the benefits. The son who comes of two strong parents will be strong also, and perhaps even a good ruler. I presume that is what you want for your people." Or you are a bad king as well as a bad father, I thought. It was not necessary to say this; I knew he understood.

"As for the suitors agreeing to it," I went on, "they will."

I had rehearsed my next words with care.

"The arrogant will leap at the chance to win against me," I said. "They will be thinking only of the fame such a feat will bring, not the consequences of failure. The infatuated," I went on, as if they had often wearied me, "will happily risk their lives for love."

He was looking at me differently now, like someone roused from sleep by a deadly assassin.

I bade them good night.

Artemis: Amazing.

Apollo: Your quiver, please.

Artemis: Holy Hera! I'll never bet against her again.

Apollo: Too bad. I've been coveting your obsidian knife.

Artemis: Enough! I'm going hunting.

Apollo: Don't shoot too many helpless little animals. You're supposed to protect them, remember?

Artemis: Be quiet, won't you!

Apollo: Sore loser.

PART THREE

The Races

SEVENTEEN

Aphrodite: Eros, peel me a grape.

Eros: I'm busy, Mother.

Aphrodite: Do as I say, darling, and I'll let you shoot someone for me. Don't you want to make some poor, unsuspecting mortal fall in love?

Eros: Here's your grape.

Aphrodite: Thank you, my sweet. Now, do you know where Arcadia is?

It was Perifanos who told me about the race. We were riding—I had implored him to take me out, and gruff Mataios had given permission—and I had just had my first extended gallop on Callisto. Perifanos did not object when I asked to go at speed; he could see that I was surer of my balance now.

Crouching atop Callisto with her mane whipping my face, overtaking and then passing Perifanos' big bay, I was happier than I had been since coming to the palace.

The euphoria ended far too quickly. When we slowed to a trot and Perifanos caught up with us, he told me that I would be racing my first suitor the following day.

My heart slammed. "Tomorrow?" I managed to ask. "How do you know?"

"Mataios heard it from Pistos." The old man who served wine at dinner was also my father's personal attendant.

I reminded myself that Perifanos, like Pistos, was in my father's employ, and that my father must think I was eager to race. "Who hastens here so eagerly to meet his death?" I asked lightly, as if I were asking what meats would be served at dinner. Yet the thought of what lay ahead sickened me. How could anyone come forward knowing the conditions I had set?

Wholly disheartened, I looked down at the reins in my hand. The threat of death—a strategy I had thought so ingenious, so wonderfully clever—had not kept anyone away, and now I would have to kill a man. It was horrible, like being wrapped in a poisonous cloak of my own design.

"I do not know," said Perifanos.

No matter, I thought. My father would be quite pleased to tell me.

Perifanos watched me impassively. If he sensed my distress, he gave no sign. "Another gallop?" he asked.

"As long as it's not back to the palace."

This made him smile.

"Thank you for telling me about tomorrow," I said. Before he could reply, I urged Callisto forward.

It took him a long time to catch us.

EIGHTEEN

Entella brought up the race while she arranged my hair before dinner. I was not surprised. Entella knew everything that went on in the palace, from who dented the king's goblet (Pistos, who had dared to blame it on her daughter Agnos) to what Nephele took for her monthly headaches (feverfew).

"Your first suitor!" she exclaimed, as her hands braided tirelessly. "Well! Who is he?"

"I was going to ask you that," I said.

"Me!" She feigned surprise.

"You might have heard something," I replied blandly, "from Pistos, or Nephele."

"Pistos never tells me anything," she said. "He stopped

when your mother died. I said some things about the king. . . . Pistos is very loyal to him."

"And Nephele?"

"The Lady Nephele knows only what the king tells her." From the way she said it, I guessed it was very little. Poor Nephele, I thought.

"Did my father love my mother?" I had wanted to ask this from the time Entella had told me about my mother's death.

"What a question!" she exclaimed, this time with genuine surprise.

I shrugged. "You must know," I said. If the answer did not come from Entella, it would not come at all, for I would never ask my father.

"He did love her," she said slowly, and with great conviction. "He loved her dearly." Her hands slowed. "One day when they were newly married, I saw him do something—I was just a girl, but I have never forgotten it."

I bowed my head, waiting.

"Your mother was at the gates, on her horse. They were saying goodbye. Just before she rode away, your father leaned over and kissed her leg."

I tried to picture it and could not.

"The look they exchanged made me blush," she said, "all the way down to my toes."

"So they were happy?" The words cost me effort.

"At first."

She would not say it, so I did. "Until I was born."

Her hands stopped, settling on my shoulders. She had a warm, kindly touch, and I was grateful for it. I let my head fall back so that it rested on her bosom. I had no memories of my infancy, only Castor's account of finding me, alone and naked, in a she-bear's den. "You looked like a fat, filthy grub," he liked to say, "with cheeks pink from howling." He would always add, "thanks to the goddess," but it was years before I knew why.

At length Entella said, "She could not forgive him. And he would not let her leave."

But she found a way, I thought. I closed my eyes against the hot sting of tears and saw my mother's horse picking its way back to the palace. What had my father felt, I wondered, when it appeared without her? Grief? Remorse? Rage? Fear? Whatever it was, I thought, it had not changed him. He was a tyrant then, and he was a tyrant now.

A defiant voice inside me said, do not let him crush you.

I took a deep breath. "Entella," I said, "I need poison. Can you find some for me?"

"Oh!" This was almost a shriek, and Aura, who lay at my feet, started in alarm. "How can you ask me such a thing?" cried Entella. "I will not help you take your own life!"

"No, no," I protested, "you misunderstand. The poison is not for me—it is for my opponent."

"Your opponent? What opponent?" She was so agitated that beads of sweat appeared on her upper lip.

"Please, calm yourself," I said, forcing her to sit. "I will explain why I need it, if you will only listen."

She dried her face on her hem. When her bosom stopped heaving, I said, "I do not wish to marry. My father insists on it. So I have set conditions. That is why I am racing."

"And the poison—?"

"You have not heard?" I asked. She shook her head. So Pistos has been quiet, I thought, surprised. "My suitors must race me," I told her. "Those who lose must die."

"Die?" She was incredulous.

I nodded unhappily. "No man can outrun me," I said. "I have proved it many times. Some have even called me"—I lowered my voice, lest the gods take offense—"the swiftest mortal alive.

"I thought my reputation would keep suitors away. I was wrong. It seems the threat of death is alluring." I grimaced.

"And now I must honor the conditions I set." I thought of Castor, who had taught me that honor was keeping one's word. What would he make of these happenings? I wondered. I would give a great deal to know.

"You are so determined not to marry?" asked Entella.

"Yes."

"Why?"

"I have my reasons." After a moment I said, "I was always told that the goddess Artemis saved my life. I took a vow of chastity in her honor years ago. Before I came here she sent me a sign, a warning against marriage. I cannot ignore it." Entella's solemn expression told me she understood, and I was grateful.

"I thought offering poison would be . . . kinder." As soon as I said this, it sounded foolish and stupid to me. Death was death.

"Will you help me?" I pleaded, taking her hand. "You are the only one I can ask."

When she hesitated, I said, "I do not want to cause

anyone's death. But if the first dies, the others may stay away. That is my hope."

She squeezed my hand and told me she would do what she could. Her words so reassured me that I felt easier about hearing my father's announcement, which came promptly after his third glass of wine.

NINETEEN

I took the news calmly. "Tomorrow?" I echoed, wiping my hands daintily on my chiton. We were eating goat. "Good. A run will be welcome." As far as I knew, my father was ignorant of my predawn excursions.

"Mataios tells me you have been riding," he said.

"Have you?" Nephele looked at me wide-eyed. She was the kind of soft, fluttery woman who feared all four-legged creatures but kittens.

"I hope you don't mind," I replied. "It is very diverting."

"Not at all." I watched him drink, wondering if he thought of my mother when he heard of my affection for horses. I hoped so. For a moment I seethed with dark, vengeful thoughts.

115

"I am sure the race tomorrow will be diverting also," he said. "Particularly as you know your suitor. Or so he claims."

"Oh? Who is he?"

"Cepheus. He says he was on the Hunt with you."

"Cepheus!" I nearly spat out my food.

"You do know him, then."

Well enough, I thought with dislike, seeing his close-set eyes and perpetual sneer. "Why has he come forward?" I demanded.

"He says he loves you," said my father, smiling at my loss of composure. "Can he be lying?"

"Why would he lie?" asked Nephele.

"He hates me!" I said. "When his friend Ancaeus was killed on the Hunt, Cepheus held me responsible."

"Then why would he want to marry you?" inquired my father.

"Perhaps he is deranged," I said. "Ancaeus' death may have pushed him into madness. Grief drives people to extremes," I added pointedly, "as you know."

116

My father blinked. Otherwise ignoring the reference to my mother, he said, "He seems rational enough. Most definitely in his right mind. Healthy, too." He cocked his head. "He looks as strong as a bull."

You are disgusting, I thought. "Crazed or sane, it makes no difference," I said, rising. "The man is slow on his feet."

I went back to my chamber and wept.

TWENTY

I ran the next morning. When I was deep in the forest, at my rough shrine, I made an offering and prayed. I asked Artemis to watch over me. I dedicated the race to her. I requested a merciful death for Cepheus. Then I ended my prayer as I always did, with the words "I am yours."

Apollo: A small wager, sister?

Artemis: We both know she'll win.

Apollo: True. Too bad victory comes at such a price.

Artemis: Her decision.

Apollo: She made it because of you.

Artemis: You sent her the dreams.

Apollo: Have you no mercy? She's in a terrible predicament!

Artemis: She can handle it. If she couldn't, I'd still have my ivory quiver, wouldn't I?

The course was short, about sixteen acres. It began far below the walls, at the point where the ground leveled, and followed the narrow footpath that encircled the palace. My father had taken the trouble to have the path widened, smoothed, and spread with sand, niceties that surprised me. Perhaps he imagined many such races.

May the gods forbid it, I thought.

I wore a short chiton, and now I tucked the small horn vial of poison inside my belt. Entella had told me the stuff was deadly and swift. "The faster the better," I had said, wishing the morning were over.

A small crowd waited near the course—guards, servants, and a few others I had come to know, like Mataios, Perifanos, and Pistos. Entella was there with little Agnos and Galini, the daughters who helped her in the kitchen.

My father and Nephele had not yet arrived, though chairs had been set out for them.

I remembered Cepheus' characteristic expression as somewhere between a glower and a sneer, but when he saw me, he simply stared, and kept on staring as I came down the hill. He left his companions, four well-oiled, muscular young men, to join me near the track.

"Greetings, Atalanta," he said loudly, fixing me with his dark, close-set eyes. He looked unusually clean, I thought, but then the last time I had seen him he had been drenched in boar's blood.

"Greetings, Cepheus," I replied. "I am surprised to find you here."

He swallowed several times before replying, and a flush crept up his thick neck. "I am surprised also," he confessed. Then he made an abrupt, harsh, braying sound that could only be laughter. "And I will be surprised if I win this race," he went on, "but I—I could not stay away."

Here was a Cepheus I did not know—awkward, bewildered, almost humble. Great gods on the mountain, I thought, looking away, what is he trying to tell me? At this moment my father appeared. He was as pale as a specter, and so weak that Nephele and Mataios had to help him into his high-backed chair.

"I see that you two are renewing your friendship," he said approvingly.

Friendship! I thought. That is not what I would call it.

He settled himself and looked out at the crowd, which quickly fell silent. "You are witnesses to this race," he announced in his deep voice, "between my daughter Atalanta, and Prince Cepheus of Arcadia. If the prince wins, he and Atalanta will marry. If Atalanta wins, the prince will die."

There was an audible intake of breath. Some spectators, it seemed, were hearing the terms of the contest for the first time.

My father looked over at us. He raised a skeletal hand. "At my signal," he said.

We crouched. I could feel Cepheus staring but kept my eyes resolutely on my father's hand until it fell. Then I began to run at a very moderate pace. Cepheus charged forward, pumping his arms and scrambling into the lead, a feat that drew loud acclamation from his friends. I let him stay ahead as we took the first turn at the southwest corner of the palace. I had no desire to humiliate him.

As we ran north, there were cries from above. The stable boys were atop the walls screaming encouragement, their voices as high and piercing as the whistles they used to summon the horses from the fields.

"Faster, Princess, faster!" called Koris. "Don't trot, gallop!" I waved to him. A few of the guards stationed on the wall called out to Cepheus, who was able to maintain his speed as we started uphill.

I caught up to him just past the northwest corner. It was the point at which the track fell behind the palace, and where we would be visible only to those on the wall. Even they, however, could not hear what we said.

"Cepheus," I called, loping beside him. He turned, and there was such naked hope on his face that my gut clenched with pity. He actually thought I might let him win.

I held out the vial. "Take it," I said. "Quickly!" When it was in his hand, I told him what it was. He was too breathless to speak, but he shook his head once, violently, and threw down the vial without breaking stride.

I retrieved it and caught up to him. "Please take it!" I begged. "There isn't much time." We would soon round the third, northeast corner, where the final stretch began. I lay my hand on his broad forearm, and for a moment he slowed. I could feel the blood pumping beneath his skin.

"It is best this way," I told him, hating the empty words. In truth, the poison was just as much for me as for him; I could not bear to see him strangled, or beheaded. I was overcome with such self-loathing that I shuddered.

There was fear in his eyes now, and he was panting too heavily to reply. The sound he made was awful, like tree limbs groaning in winter wind.

I pressed the vial into his hand. "I am sorry," I said.

Then I ran to my victory.

TWENTY-ONE

Aphrodite: You shot the wrong person, you naughty boy!

Eros: I did?

Aphrodite: Stop giggling. You know Atalanta was meant to be your target.

Eros: Sorry.

Aphrodite: You're not, but never mind. You'll have another chance very soon.

My next suitor—a Cretan prince in ringlets and gold earrings—arrived two days later. Many silk-clad young men came with him, chattering amongst themselves as if they were attending a court celebration rather than a contest with a truly terrible second prize.

The prince could neither speak nor understand our

dialect, but one of his friends knew a little Achaean. Whispering and gesticulating, he attempted to translate my father's words to the crowd. I do not think he succeeded, for when the speech ended, the prince and his party looked entertained rather than apprehensive.

I offered the poison midrace, but my efforts to tell the prince what it was and why he should take it failed. When at last I simply pressed the vial into his hand, he smiled as if I had given him a love token. I ran the final lap wishing that I were far, far away from my father and his noxious demands.

Three others came after the Cretan prince. I won against them all. I began to feel like an executioner, and thought often of my childhood fascination with tales of human sacrifice in Arcadia. Whispered talk of men hunted like stags, throats cut, and strange prayers uttered had once thrilled and horrified me, in the way that cruelty excites the young.

But my own experience of human sacrifice, for that is how I came to view the races, did not thrill me in any way.

126

Rather, I felt a constant dull nausea. The knowledge that in keeping my word I was pleasing no one—not the gods, not my father, and least of all my suitors—was truly sickening.

My daily prayers to the goddess had once given me comfort; now they were dreary. I wanted the races to end. I wanted the suitors to stay away, as I had always meant them to. I wanted the goddess to intervene on my behalf. My desperation and self-pity were unworthy of her, yet I expressed them time and again. I had never known such dismal confusion.

Then Entella told me she was running out of poison.

Aphrodite: I heard the prayers of the nicest young man today. He's called Hippomenes, and he's madly in love with Atalanta.

Eros: Ha! He's doomed.

Aphrodite: He was so sweet. He did a full prostration.

Eros: Facedown on the ground?

Aphrodite: Yes! I haven't seen one in ages, have you?

Eros: No.

Aphrodite: It quite won me over. So few mortals show the proper humility when they supplicate, have you noticed?

Eros: I've never been supplicated, Mother. It's you they implore and beseech, not me.

Aphrodite: Nonsense. At any rate, Hippomenes nearly wept with gratitude when I gave him the three golden apples.

Eros: Apples? What for?

Aphrodite: To throw ahead of Atalanta when they race. She'll stop to pick them up, and he'll run ahead of her. Clever, no?

Eros: What if she doesn't stop?

Aphrodite: That's where you come in, my precious.

TWENTY-TWO

Two days, then three, went by without a single suitor. I rambled around the palace with Aura, rode Callisto, and entertained the wild hope that all young men rash enough to race me had already done so. Perhaps the rest had been frightened away.

I began to think of returning to my people, that it might just be possible if there were no more races. In that event, how could my father object? He might even be glad to see his troublesome daughter go, and what a fine thing that would be, I thought, to bid him farewell victoriously.

I wondered if he would let me keep Callisto.

Then his health declined and he took to his bed. In his absence the meals I shared with Nephele were almost dreamily serene, punctuated by little grunts of satisfaction rather than conversation.

This peaceful interlude ended on the fifth day, when Entella reported that my father was feeling better. "He left his bed this noon," she said.

"Ah." I must have slumped, for her next words were, "Please raise your head, my lady, so I can finish your hair."

I sat up. "Will he dine with us tonight?" I asked.

"Yes."

Thus warned, I prepared myself for more of my father's dinnertime despotism, the silky animosity, the fitful drunken outbursts. But I was not prepared for his appearance—he was pale to the point of transparency—nor his first words.

"Another suitor comes tomorrow," he told me, "and he will be your last."

"Why is that?"

"Because I am sick to death of these delays! I am the king! You will obey me!"

"And if I do not?"

"There will be consequences!" He hit the table with all the force he could muster, and his heavy gold rings clinked against the wood.

"My lord, please!" entreated Nephele.

He ignored her. "Dire consequences," he raged.

I thought of my mother, hanging from a tree. "Dire consequences!" I repeated. "Would you drive *me* to suicide, as well?" His eyes grew wider and his mouth moved as if he would speak, but he did not.

I got to my feet. "If there is a man who can outrun me, I will wed him. If no such man appears, I will remain chaste. That is my vow. I have made it to Artemis as well as you, and I will keep it. I must keep it," I added, "for I owe her my life—the life she saved when you tried to kill me."

Nephele made a sound of distress. She was staring at my father in disbelief. He had managed, somehow, to avoid telling her the truth about me. Hearing it now, she stared at him open-mouthed, waiting for a denial or an explanation.

Again he said nothing.

"Artemis is the goddess of childbirth," I said. "If she wishes you to have an heir, you will have one. If not, your line will end with me."

Apollo: I think I'm falling in love.

Artemis: Oh, stop.

Apollo: I pity her next suitor. Actually, I pity all her suitors.

Artemis: What a sorry lot. And they keep coming! They try and try and try, when it's perfectly clear that they'll lose!

Apollo: That's what mortals do.

Artemis: Remind me never to take divinity for granted.

TWENTY-THREE

There were few spectators the next day—two shepherds, some ragged children, Entella and her daughters, and the ever-faithful stable boys, who perched restlessly atop the palace walls like big, unruly birds.

I was impatient for the race to start, only because I wanted it to be over, and saw with annoyance that my father and Nephele had not yet appeared. I looked around for my opponent. Almost always the suitors came with companions, court friends who dispensed urgently whispered advice and hearty slaps of encouragement before the race. But today there was no such ensemble. Instead, I saw a lone figure standing under a tree, a tall, broad-shouldered, fair-haired young man.

He was watching me. His golden brown eyes did not

waver as he approached, but held mine. Just as I was thinking that he was remarkably self-possessed for someone who was about to die, I felt a piercing blow to my heart. I had seen men shot by arrows, the way they staggered and doubled over with pain. I could see no arrow, yet I had felt one. I whimpered in fright, staggering a little. With the blow my dull nausea sharpened, overpowering me, and I retched.

Undeterred, the young man offered his hand. "Princess," he said.

He was extremely handsome.

I shook my downcast head, backing away unsteadily. I could not reply; my throat was convulsing, and my mouth was filling with spittle. I am going to vomit! I thought frantically. What has happened to me?

I spat; at this he jumped back.

"Atalanta! What ails you?" This was my father, who had arrived in a chair borne by four attendants. He sounded both petulant and suspicious, as if he thought I was feigning illness to avoid the race.

Suddenly I remembered Zoi's words to me at Gortys. She had told me I would suffer a wound some time in the future. Had I just been wounded? I ran my hands up and down my arms. My skin was intact, but I could swear by the goddess that I had been shot.

Nephele hurried to my side. "Are you ill?" she asked.

"No," I blurted, acutely aware of my bare-chested suitor. He stood close to me, giving off the scent of clove. It was very pleasant. I took a deep breath.

"Are you certain?" she pressed.

"I am," I said, and I was. For my nausea was gone, taking with it every worry, care, vile preoccupation, and misgiving that had been crowding my mind. Suddenly I felt as bright and weightless as a glint of sunlight.

I placed my hand on Nephele's shoulder. "I am," I repeated, willing her to return to my father. She did.

Now I noticed that the young man's watchful, amber eyes were slightly uptilted, that his generous, well-defined mouth had an upward curve of immense charm, and that his complexion was unusually tawny for someone with such fair hair.

His skin looked very smooth. I yearned to touch it so badly that my fingers twitched.

"I am Hippomenes," he said.

"Atalanta," I replied.

"I know that." He smiled.

I flushed. "Of course you do," I managed.

"It is good to see you again."

"Again?"

"I—I have watched you, and thought about you," he said, "ever since the boar hunt in Calydon."

"The Hunt? You were there?" I wondered how I had failed to notice him.

He nodded. "I saw you hit the boar. It was an unforgettable sight. You looked so . . . invincible."

Remembering, I grimaced. "That is not how I felt," I said.

Hippomenes regarded me gravely for a moment. Then he

said, "Meleager's uncles behaved very badly. They were the elders. They should have shown restraint." No one had thought to say this to me before; I had hardly been able to think it. Hearing the words, I felt both relief and gratitude. Who are you? I yearned to ask Hippomenes. How do you know me so well?

It was at this moment that my father chose to begin his address. I had heard his speech often enough so that I could give it myself, but now, as he concluded with the familiar words, "If Atalanta wins, the prince must die," I stopped breathing.

Die? I thought, appalled. I glanced over at Hippomenes. He crouched in readiness, muscles taut, eyes on the track.

"At my signal," called my father.

* * *

Eros: This should be good.

Apollo: She'll win. She always wins.

Eros: Maybe not. I think she's smitten. Did you see the way she was looking at him?

Apollo: She looked the way she always looks—determined.

Eros: How about a small wager? I say she loses.

Apollo: You're too young to gamble. Besides, you don't have anything I want.

Eros: I have forgetfulness powder, and elixir of convulsive lust.

Apollo: Do you? Hmm. The powder sounds good.

Eros: Zeus uses it on Hera all the time. One little sprinkle, and she forgets she's a jealous wife.

Apollo: Really! That sounds very useful.

Eros: It never fails. Anyway, if I bet the powder, what will you bet? How about that quiver?

Apollo: This? I don't know . . . it's such a handsome thing.

Eros: So you *are* afraid she'll lose.

Apollo: All right, the quiver.

He had long legs and a stride to match, and made a good, fast start when my father's hand came down. Not a bad runner, I thought, catching up to him without difficulty. I ran alongside him for the first stretch, which seemed shorter than I remembered.

No words passed between us, but we were close, and for the moment, alone. I stole a glance at him as we took the first turn. He was looking at me. When our eyes caught, I could not help but smile.

We began to run uphill and he fell back. I slowed a little, moving to the outside and shortening my stride. It would be tricky to regulate the distance between us so that it did not grow, I thought; speeding up was so much easier. I was not accustomed to reducing my pace. Until now, I had always run to win.

I put myself just far enough ahead of him so that I could hear his breathing.

Something shot past me, shimmering in the air like a bit of rainbow. It fell to the ground directly in my path and lay there, glowing. Its muzzy radiance lured me like a song.

Even thinking, Go on! Keep running! I could not. I stopped
and picked it up.

It was an apple made of gold.

Artemis: What in holy Hades is that?

Apollo: I don't know. But she's taking a long time to look at
it. Blast! He's running ahead, and she's just standing there!
She'll lose the race if she doesn't hurry!

Artemis: Hmm. Odd.

Apollo: Do something! Tell her to run!

Artemis: Maybe I will. And maybe I won't.

TWENTY-FOUR

I turned the apple slowly in my hand. It was an enchanting thing—heavy, warm to the touch, its greenish gold surface textured with all the dots and speckles and tiny bumps of a real apple. It even gave off a faint perfume. But when I sniffed it, I smelled not apple, but clove.

Clove, I thought. Hippomenes smelled of clove. Had he thrown it? I sniffed it again; my nose wrinkled in pleasure. I lifted the golden fruit to my mouth, intending to taste it, and heard the steady beat of footsteps.

Hippomenes ran past me, casting a quick glance my way. I stood there holding the apple, admiring his muscular back and his wide, elegant shoulder blades as he ran up the incline of the second stretch. It occurred to me that I had never before seen a man who looked as good from the back as from the front, and that this was—in its way—a most appealing quality.

"Run, Princess! Run!" Screeching like jays, the stable boys atop the palace wall startled me into motion. Tucking the apple into my belt—and feeling, with a shock, the vial of poison—I took the uphill stretch at speed, coming abreast of Hippomenes at the second turning.

There I slowed sharply, and for a moment or two we ran along the back wall in tandem. When his breathing grew labored, I came down to a walk, then stopped. Suddenly we were almost touching.

I looked up at him. "Thank you for the apple," I said. "It is beautiful."

He struggled to catch his breath. On his heaving chest, a trickle of sweat meandered down toward his navel, then disappeared into a fine line of golden hair.

"You are welcome," he replied, and we stood there looking at each other. It was an oddly comforting moment, like the time I had first entered the cave at Gortys. I had felt then as if I were returning to a much-loved, long-forgotten place. Here, with Hippomenes, I felt the same.

Sparrows trilled. Aphrodite's bird, I thought absently. It occurred to me that the Goddess of Love had never once appeared to me, in dreams or otherwise. The sparrows trilled again, until the air chimed with their sweet, liquid call.

Hippomenes took my hand. "Marry me," he said.

The stable boys came skittering along the top of the wall, drowning out the birdsong with their shouts. They had seen me slow my pace on this stretch before, seen me exchange words with other suitors. I suspected that they might even know about the poison. But they had never seen me stop, much less permit a suitor to touch me, and there was a note of alarm in their cries.

They do not know what to make of this, I thought. Nor do I.

Then my skin prickled, the way it sometimes did before a storm, and a tremor shook the air. It shook me, too, so that I knew the goddess was near. She has come to speed me along, I thought, and for the first time in my life I was afraid of her.

I withdrew my hand from Hippomenes. "Only if you win the race," I said, a little more loudly than was necessary.

Then I took flight.

TWENTY-FIVE

I had scarcely gone ten paces when I saw a streak of gold fly past me like an arrow. It was a second apple from Hippomenes. This one fell far from the track, rolling all the way to the forest's edge. It would take much longer to retrieve than the first. I ran to it as if pulled.

It lay beaming in a clump of ferns, and seemed to brighten as I picked it up. Its yellow-gold surface was adorned with flecks and speckles and even a tiny wormhole, and when I sniffed it, I again smelled clove. I rubbed the apple dreamily against my cheek, turning it this way and that in my best imitation of wonder, and listened for Hippomenes.

At last I heard his footsteps.

Slow, too slow, I thought, as he passed me by. He was a strong runner by ordinary standards, but no match for me, and of all those watching the race, Artemis knew this best. She, who must believe I was trying to win, had seen me run at twice this speed for my own amusement. If she suspected the truth—that I was allowing Hippomenes to overtake me—she would never smile on me again.

I could live without her favor, I thought, but inciting her displeasure was something else entirely. I had seen enough of her cruel, implacable anger on the Hunt to last me for the rest of my life. I quailed at the thought of becoming its target.

Yet death was cruel and implacable also, I thought, tucking the second apple into my waist. If the goddess had her way, I would win this race just as I had won the others, and death would take Hippomenes, too. It was a heinous thought.

I reached the track just as he rounded the turn onto the final stretch. I could close the gap between us with little effort, but I did not; I held steady.

His pace increased. This was a surprise; I had not

thought him capable of greater speed. Helped by the downhill slope, he ran even faster.

I fought my urge to lengthen my stride.

Then, perhaps spurred to greater effort by the sight of the finish post, he ran faster still, and the gap between us grew.

I could see my father in the distance, sternly upright in his chair, and wondered if he was steeling himself for yet another defeat. Probably. In every other race, I had run at a moderate pace until the midpoint of the final stretch, the one Hippomenes was about to pass. Then I would truly hurry, running so fast that my hair flew straight behind me like a stick, or so Entella said. Finishing this way, in a sudden, ferocious burst of speed, I would reach the post far ahead of my opponent. After I won, I liked to walk over to my father, stand before him, and look steadily into his eyes for a moment before I strode away.

He could not suspect that today would be different, I thought. How could he?

Then Hippomenes threw another golden apple.

Eros: She's slowing down! She's going to follow the apple!

Aphrodite: Those apples were such an inspiration, if I do say so myself. And you shot her, too, didn't you, darling?

Eros: Let's keep that a secret.

Aphrodite: Why?

Eros: No special reason. Look! There goes Hippomenes!

Yet another one, I thought. He is persistent!

The third apple was red-gold, gaudy and beautiful against the blue of the sky. It came down slowly, as if choosing where to land, then hit the earth about a hundred paces away, and set off toward a dry stream bed. Hippomenes was nearly at the finish post. If I chased this apple, as I had chased the others, I would have to push very hard to overtake him.

I might actually lose the race.

That's what you want, isn't it? I asked myself, and the

question stopped me like a wall. I had never lost a race; now that the possibility was upon me, I clutched my sides in panic. My right hand touched something small and unyielding through the folds of cloth at my waist. Puzzled, I ran my fingers over it.

Poison. The merciful death I provided for my suitors.

No more of this, I thought, plucking the vial from my waistband and casting it away. No more!

I did not want to lose. Even less, however, did I want Hippomenes to die.

Apollo: What did *she* just throw?

Artemis: The poison.

Apollo: Really? Then give her another push!

Artemis: It won't do any good.

Apollo: What do you mean?

Artemis: Girls of her age often behave this way. They're chaste, they're pure, they're utterly devoted, and then, in a blink, they change. Suddenly I'm part of their childhood, like a discarded toy. . . . I could have sworn she'd be different, but why should she be?

Apollo: I'm not sure I understand you.

Artemis: Have you seen Eros around here recently?

Apollo: Aphrodite's son? Now that you mention it . . . yes, he's been around.

Artemis: He shot her.

Apollo: Atalanta? You think so?

Artemis: Why else would she let Hippomenes take the lead? She's in love.

Apollo: Eros shot her?

Artemis: I'd swear to it. He looks sweet and harmless, but those golden arrows of his are surprisingly potent. Sometimes their effect lasts for years.

Apollo: Blast that pudgy little toad! He tricked me!

Artemis: Tricked you? How?

Apollo: Never mind. Oh, look! There goes Atalanta!

TWENTY-SIX

I chased the apple and then I chased my suitor. As I drew closer to him, I remembered Zoi's prediction on the beach at Gortys, that poets would sing of my strength, and my courage, and my wild spirit. Her words had amazed me, for I had often yearned for glory, but secretly and without hope. Only men were heroes, never women; it had always been so. Zoi had made me think that would change.

Will the poets sing of me if I lose? I wondered, coming abreast of Hippomenes. Then I thought, They will if they are clever. Win or lose, it makes a good story.

I fell into step with Hippomenes and we ran side by side, as we had at the start of the race. But now he was breathing so hard that his mouth was agape, and his eyes were wide with effort and fear. He looked like a hunted stag. We were almost at the finish post, and he could see that I was running entirely without strain. It would be easy for me to pull ahead even now, and he knew it.

Three paces from the finish I felt his eyes on me. I tilted my head so that he alone could see my face, and I smiled. Then I shortened my stride by a hand's-breadth—no, the hand's-breadth of a child—and we came to the end of the race.

Eros: I won! I won!

Aphrodite: Hippomenes won, you mean.

Eros: Yes, Hippomenes won!

Aphrodite: She certainly kept me in suspense all the way to the end. Are you sure you hit her with your arrow?

Eros: I hit her, Mother. She loves him. That's why she lost.

Aphrodite: Poor boy. He's going to have his hands full.

He took my hand and squeezed it, hard, while his chest heaved and his head came down. His wet hair clung to his neck in dark tendrils. I smelled clove and sweat. When he could speak, he whispered his thanks so passionately that I blushed. There were sparrows chirping, and a few murmurs of surprise from the crowd, but for a time I was aware of little else but Hippomenes and the feel of his hand gripping mine.

Then my father cleared his throat. He looked dumbfounded, as if I had just metamorphosed into a Cyclops. For once he was truly at a loss for words: the outcome of the race had rendered him speechless.

He is an old man, very near death, I thought, and I pitied him.

"Father," I said, stepping forward, "will you award the victor?" In case he had forgotten, I added, "He is called Hippomenes." My father recovered himself and beckoned to Hippomenes, who knelt before him.

The gathering fell silent.

"Today is an auspicious day," said my father, "and a hopeful one for our kingdom. In winning against my daughter—Atalanta, swiftest of mortals—Hippomenes has also won her hand. There will be no death today, but a celebration—a wedding feast." At this, Nephele fairly bobbed with happiness.

My father raised his voice, declaiming with mock solemnity, "You are a lucky man, Hippomenes. The gods must love you!" This drew laughter, as well as a modest shake of the head from my betrothed.

Forgive me, goddess, I thought. Be merciful.

Looking my way, my father added, "May they love you even more when Atalanta is your wife." It was his way of saying he wanted a grandson as quickly as possible, and again there was laughter.

Hippomenes cast a sidelong glance my way and my toes curled. I resolved to make an offering to Artemis without delay.

Eros: The ivory quiver, please.
Apollo: You little cheat! You shot Atalanta and made her fall in love! It wasn't a fair bet.

Eros: She lost, I won. Hand it over.

Apollo: I'm warning you, Eros, this isn't the kind of thing I take lightly. And when Artemis hears about it, she'll be furious! My sister has a hair-raising temper, you know, much worse than mine. It's as bad as Zeus'!

Eros: I'll try to remember that. And if you ever want to place another bet—

Apollo: No more bets for me.

Eros: Too bad. The stakes on whether she has a boy or a girl are going to go sky-high.

TWENTY-SEVEN

I am chaste no more, but my modesty is intact. So I will say only this of my wedding night: my father leered, Nephele wept, and Entella fussed, but Hippomenes' ardor made up for it all. I had never expected to leave my girlhood with such joy, yet I did.

As he and I lay entwined, watching the night fade away, we spoke softly of many things. He told me about his homeland, Mycenae, the great city to the east, and his family; I told him about mine. When I spoke of my mother—haltingly, for I had never done so before, save with Entella—he stroked my face.

At first light he told me of his prayers to Aphrodite, and her gift of the golden apples. "She said they would enchant you, that you would chase them because you are a woman and all women love gold. Even so, I feared you would not."

I asked why.

"Because you are not like other women," he said, stroking my cheek, "and I knew it from the moment I saw you."

"When was that?" I asked.

"When we gathered for the Hunt. You were talking with Jason, and stringing your bow. At first I thought you were a man, because of your height. Then I came closer." He took my hand. "I remember thinking you were unlike any woman I had ever seen, and more beautiful." He raised my hand to his lips and kissed it. "I feared you might disdain the apples, or that they would not interest you."

"You used them, though."

"They were all I had," he said. "I loved you and I wanted you. Aphrodite answered my prayers. When she offered her help, I could not really quibble about the form it took, could I?"

I shook my head.

"I won because you let me win," he said.

"Yes."

"Why?"

I turned. "When we first spoke, I felt as if I knew you, somehow, and that you knew me. You felt . . . familiar. The feeling grew stronger as we raced. At the end, I—I could not bear to think of you dead."

I could just see his smile in the waning dark. Presently he said, "Your father was right."

"About what?"

"I am a lucky man."

We stayed in all that day and night, attended by Galini and Agnos, who swept our chamber, sprinkled it with lavender, brought food and water at regular intervals, and never glanced at Hippomenes without blushing. I could not fault them. Still, I was always impatient for them to go, as I longed to be gazing at him or touching him myself. Even Aura, who had taken up residence on the dusty old tiger skin, was besotted. If he so much as spoke her name, her ears flew back and she scuttled over to him adoringly.

The next day he left me before dawn, and she went with

him. When they returned, she had something long and slender in her mouth. She carried it as carefully as if it were a newborn pup.

Artemis: Whatever happened to my quiver?

Apollo: Quiver? What quiver?

Artemis: The ivory one. That you won from me.

Apollo: Oh, I misplaced it. I'm sure it'll turn up.

Artemis: You lost it?

Apollo: Heavens! Just look at the sky! If I don't hitch up my chariot, sunrise will be late!

"What's that?" I asked, stretching contentedly. Sunshine flashed in the tiger's glass eye, making it wink. It was midmorning. I had been sleeping for hours.

"Something for you," said Hippomenes, urging Aura forward. She set the thing on the bed. It was a quiver of pale animal horn, edged with gold, adorned with delicate carvings of the waxing and waning moon. Two quail feathers hung from its red leather strap, which was sewn with tiny, perfectly even stitches.

I picked it up. It was as smooth and slender as a deer's shinbone, nearly weightless, and infinitely pleasing to hold.

"This is a treasure," I said, thinking I had never seen anything so finely wrought. Castor's bows, even the golden apples, paled before it. "It might have been made by Hephaestus." The smith-god's works were so beautiful that he was thought to be more of a sorcerer than a craftsman.

Hippomenes smiled. "It is worthy of you."

I thanked him with an embrace. Presently he told me that he had found the quiver in the forest, on the moss-covered banks of a stream, after offering to Eros.

"Eros!" I was surprised to hear the boy-god's name. He was a capricious, heartless creature, who took pleasure in tormenting gods and mortals alike with sudden, inexplicable passions. In his way he was more frightening than Pan, who amused himself by broadcasting fear.

"Why were you offering to him?"

"Gratitude," said Hippomenes.

I felt his watchful golden eyes on me as I took in his meaning. Two breaths, three, and I had it.

So, I thought, Zoi was right: I did suffer a wound, a powerful one. The pain I felt when I first met Hippomenes had been Eros' invisible arrow. It had pierced my heart, and I had fallen in love.

My mind struggled with this like a fish on a line. "Did you invoke him?" I asked.

He shook his head. "I only supplicated Aphrodite. The apples were hers. But the rest . . . ."

"My love for you?"

He looked stricken. "Are you angry?" he asked.

I shook my head. It was not anger but a need to be alone that caused me to dress so hastily. When I was at the door, he asked me where I was going.

"I, too, have offerings to make," I said.

TWENTY-EIGHT

Entella told me where to go, to the hill west of the palace, near Lord Zeus' sanctuary. It did not take me long to get there; I had seen the tall, lightning-riven oak many times during my morning runs. The sanctuary overlooked fields, forest, and the blue-green river Loussios, where the god had bathed as a child. Moss on the altar and a cold firepit told me the place was long out of use. But it was sacred ground, and I trod carefully.

I had never noticed the tomb before. It was not far from the oak, yet unlike the great, blasted tree, it was not a feature of the landscape. It was regal enough—its stones were large and polished and it enjoyed the same majestic view as the sanctuary—but it was set into the hillside so that it could not be seen from the palace. This made perfect sense,

I thought. My father was not one to acknowledge his short-comings. Why would he wish to be reminded of the worst mistake of his life?

I sank down before the tomb and bowed my head.

"Mother," I whispered, "I am your lost girl, Atalanta. If you grieve for me, grieve no more. I am sixteen years old, tall and strong and fast on my feet. Entella says I resemble you. Now love has come my way. That and learning to ride a horse have made me very happy.

"I hope with all my heart that these tidings bring you peace."

As I got to my feet, a dog barked in the distance. It was Aura, who covered my face with kisses when I bent to greet her. She came with me into the forest, settling nearby when I reached my shrine. It was a rough thing, a simple rock platform, but I kept it clean, and placed a flower there every day.

Now I knelt before it, palms on my knees, and composed myself as best I could.

After a time I said, "Merciful goddess, please hear me. I swore to remain chaste and I am chaste no longer. I vowed not to marry, and now I am a wife. I pledged my life to you, wanting to be yours always, yet somehow, without willing it, I have changed."

I closed my eyes. "Nevertheless," I confessed, "I am happy.

"Goddess," I said, "I never meant to offend you. I never intended to stray from your company. I will always be grateful for your mercy. And I thank you, most humbly, for allowing me to take love where I found it."

I opened my eyes, half expecting to feel her there. But the air was still and limpid, the forest hushed. I held the quiver aloft.

"Please accept this offering," I said. Then I set it on the shrine.

Artemis: I'm touched.
Apollo: You should be!

Artemis: I can't help wondering how she got the quiver, though.

Apollo: Why trouble yourself? It's yours again. That's what matters.

Artemis: I suppose you're right. Want to go hunting?

Apollo: Let's.

Aura saw Hippomenes before I did. He had stationed himself near the northwest corner of the palace and was looking first in one direction, then another, as we started downhill. She barked and charged ahead toward him. Seeing us, he began to run our way. He ignored Aura when she jumped at him, hurrying to me with such stark urgency that I froze and nearly stumbled, wondering what awful news he bore.

But he said nothing. Instead, his arms came around me hard. It was more like a grip than an embrace, harsh and convulsive as a wrestling lock, and I recoiled. Feeling this, he whispered that love had made him do what he did, that

165

if it was less than honorable, he was sorry, truly sorry. He begged my forgiveness so abjectly that I stopped resisting. Instead, I laid my head on his shoulder and stood motionless until he fell silent.

We both heaved long sighs.

Eventually I freed an arm and patted his back, feeling the smoothness between his shoulder blades, the soft curls at the base of his neck, the tense line of his jaw. He closed his eyes, and I kissed the tender places beneath them.

"There is nothing to forgive," I said, and once again he embraced me, this time gently, yet with such persuasive longing that we were soon hurrying away from the palace, seeking some soft, hidden place where we could lie together.

As we came to the sanctuary, Hippomenes reached for me. At his touch I discarded my clothing—and my girlhood piety—with ludicrous haste. In the rapture of my desire for him, I overlooked the fact that we were on sacred ground.

The gods, however, overlook nothing.

PART FOUR

The Lion's Roar

TWENTY-NINE

We live in the forest now, sleeping by day, hunting by night. Zeus changed us for defiling his sanctuary. We should have restrained ourselves that day, but we did not. Passion prevailed, we angered the Lord of all Creation, and we paid the consequences.

So now we are lions.

In air that rippled and cracked with lightning—the bolts flew around us like burning reprimands—I watched my beloved's face grow broad and blunt, saw a mane spring up around it like a dusky golden cloud, saw his long, sinewy body fall to the ground and rise up transformed. If anything, he became even more beautiful. His eyes, large and up-tilted, continued to regard me with unswerving devotion.

My metamorphosis was equally swift and painless.

We can no longer speak with words, but we manage quite well without them. Touch is its own infinite language, and we have come to understand it very well. Our other senses are much sharper also. I especially like my new ears, which turn and flick with ease, and my new nose, which is remarkably powerful. Hunting has never been more satisfying.

Of course many things were lost to us. Countless memories vanished. Those that spring up in sleep—vivid, startling pictures of another life—slip away like shadows when we wake. I remember animals best—a great, fragrant, woolly she-bear, an ugly boar, a dog, and a horse.

Sometimes I growl when dreaming of my past, and then my mate wakes me. I know when he is dreaming because his tail twitches. There are worse things than feeling his mighty tail brush my nose, so at such times I leave him in peace.

Nevertheless, I woke him yesterday—not because he was restless, but because he was sleeping very soundly, and I wanted his attention. I nudged him with my snout until at last he raised his head. Then I nipped him; this brought him fully awake. He glared at me, whiskers aflare.

Purring, I flicked my tail. At last he caught a whiff of our newborn and was on his feet to inspect her.

He bent his head to take in her scent more thoroughly. Then his golden eyes blazed, and he gave a long, full-throated roar of satisfaction, so loud that it drew twitters from the birds in the trees. It only made her burrow deeper into my side, and suck harder.

I liked her utter lack of fear, her instinct for survival.

She would be a fine hunter.

I would teach her myself.

ANCIENT GREECE CIRCA 1500 B.C.

AUTHOR'S NOTE

Little is known about Greece in the second millennium B.C., the time when I have set this story, but most sources agree that fathers of the era were free to expose unwanted female children. All the many versions of Atalanta's story begin with the harsh fact that her father cast her out to die.

Artemis' merciful intervention, Atalanta's athletic prowess, and her father's insistence that she return to the palace to marry are all constants. Hippomenes was sometimes called Melanion, but he always sought Aphrodite's help, and she always gave him three golden apples. One popular version of the myth says that Hippomenes' ruse worked, that Atalanta lost the race because she stopped to examine the apples, as any woman would. Less well known is the story of the newlyweds' transformation into lions. It is sometimes an angry Zeus, sometimes an offended Aphrodite or Demeter who wreaks the change, but it is always intended as severe punishment.

Other, more obscure versions of Atalanta's story have her joining the quest for the Golden Fleece with Jason (and being healed of serpent-battling wounds by Medea); or going straight from the Calydonian Boar Hunt to King Pelias' funeral games, where she competed against the greatest wrestler of the age, and won. She was a daring character.

She was also, seemingly, capable of great cruelty. Her insistence on death for slow suitors appears almost bloodthirsty, yet it can also be seen as a desperate ploy to remain in Artemis' good graces. The goddess insisted on chastity, and Atalanta vowed it. As the swiftest mortal alive, she very well might have hoped that no man would be foolish enough to challenge her. If, thinking only of pleasing Artemis, she failed to imagine that Aphrodite might intervene, we cannot fault her. The immortal gods did as they pleased and were accountable only to each other.

ABOUT THE GODS

Readers unfamiliar with Greek mythology may like to know a bit more about the gods who appear in Atalanta's story. Zeus, Artemis, Apollo, and Aphrodite are all part of the original pantheon said to rule from Mount Olympus. The others are Hera, Zeus' wife; Athena, his solemn, wise, virginal daughter; Ares, God of War; Demeter, Goddess of the Harvest; Dionysus, exuberant God of Wine and intoxication; Hephaestus, God of Fire; Hermes, the fleet messenger-god; and Poseidon, Zeus' brother and Lord of all the Oceans. Eros appeared later but figured prominently in many of the myths.

Like so many divine rulers, the gods are related.

Zeus, Lord of all Creation and mighty wielder of thunderbolts, was zealously paternal, producing children whenever and wherever he could. Among the many were Apollo and Artemis and (with a different mother) Aphrodite. Zeus' wife, Hera, was notoriously jealous, with good reason.

Artemis the Huntress was a forest goddess and protector of wild animals. Rigorously chaste, she oversaw women in childbirth, as well as young girls making the transition from childhood to womanhood. Her attributes, and her association with the moon, indicate that she was absorbed into the Greek pantheon from an older culture, probably Cretan.

Apollo, Lord of the Silver Bow, God of Prophecy, healing-god and inventor of music, was Artemis' younger twin, but very unlike her. Apollo often fell in love—with both mortal women and nymphs. He fathered many children (including the great healer Asclepius), opposed barbarism, and maintained that moderation in all things was best.

Aphrodite, Goddess of Love and Zeus' daughter, was beautiful, seductive, and extremely popular: she oversaw the sexual initiation of women. Aphrodite's arranged marriage to the lame smithy Hephaestus was not altogether happy. She took many lovers, including a wide sampling of the pantheon.

Eros, Aphrodite's son, was a capricious boy whose invisible golden arrows had the power to inspire love in their targets. He shot both gods and mortals without plan, but with devastating accuracy, and was greatly feared.

A FAST-PACED FLIGHT THROUGH ANCIENT GREEK MYTHOLOGY

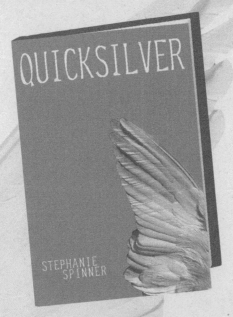

Hermes, messenger to the gods, has many talents. Wearing his famed winged sandals, he leads the dead down to Hades, and practices his favorite arts of trickery and theft. He sees the future, travels invisibly, loves jokes, and abhors violence. Follow his story of magic and mischief from Medusa's cave to Trojan War battlefields to the mysterious Underworld.

AVAILABLE WHEREVER BOOKS ARE SOLD.

www.stephaniespinner.com
www.randomhouse.com/teens

019

A FAST-PACED FLIGHT THROUGH
ANCIENT GREEK MYTHOLOGY